Praise for Samantha Sommersby's
Forbidden: The Temptation

"Jake is the ideal tortured hero, trying to come to terms with himself and his inner beast. Allison's character complements him perfectly. It's a good plot with a bit of danger, and enticing sexual chemistry brings it all together."

~ *RT Book Reviews*℠

"This [book] packs a punch from the fast loving to the eventual outcome of the crazed rogue wolf, this book does not let up!"

~ *Examiner.com*℠

"Steamy and unashamed...lots of sex, drama, and blood."

~ *Morbid Romantic*

"Forbidden: The Temptation has all the right ingredients for a compelling read."

~ *Sensual Reads*

"Sexy, arousing and hot, I was completely pulled in..."

~ *Joyfully Reviewed*

"Ms. Sommersby writes some of the best dialogue there is and never fails to turn up the heat. I loved the witty banter and sexual chemistry…"

~ *Whipped Cream Reviews*

Look for these titles by
Samantha Sommersby

Now Available:

The Forbidden Series
Forbidden: The Sacrifice
Forbidden: The Ascension
Forbidden: The Revolution
Forbidden: The Temptation

Shelter from the Storm

Forbidden:
The Temptation

Samantha Sommersby

SAMHAIN
PUBLISHING

Samhain Publishing, Ltd.
577 Mulberry Street, Suite 1520
Macon, GA 31201
www.samhainpublishing.com

Forbidden: The Temptation
Copyright © 2011 by Samantha Sommersby
Print ISBN: 978-1-60504-859-8
Digital ISBN: 978-1-60504-866-6

Editing by Tera Kleinfelter
Cover by Mandy M. Roth

This book has been previously published and has been revised and expanded from its original release.
First Samhain Publishing, Ltd. electronic publication: March 2010
First Samhain Publishing, Ltd. print publication: January 2011

Dedication

For my goddaughter, Emily. I'm so proud of the woman you've become. Enjoy college and all of the adventures that await you. Remember, this is a work of fiction. In real life, you should stay away from the boys who run naked through the woods and howl at the moon.

Chapter One

I'd never felt so free, so wild, so connected. The full moon was still a few days away, but I was strong, stronger than I'd ever been. I was at ease. Calm. My mind blissfully empty. My heart unburdened. Here, under the open sky, everything seemed simple. I just needed to let go and follow my instincts. We were on the hunt. I'd always been a good hunter. I'd had years of practice growing up. But the rules were different now. I was wolf. *Were.* Everything was different now.

The forest sped by in a blur as I continued my pursuit. With each passing second the snow fell harder, a thick layer of fresh powder accumulating on top of the hard pack. The wind picked up, whistling through the trees, creating a melody that was both comforting and haunting.

We broke through a cluster of tall pines and raced across a clearing. Mireya, Ryan and Wright were with me. Though Ryan and I were about the same age, he'd been born a lycanthrope and had grown up in the pack. To me, this was all still relatively new. I officially joined the pack last summer, but since then I'd spent little of it in their company, as Mireya was always quick to remind me. She was our female Beta and, as such, it was her job to ease me into my new life. I hadn't been making it easy for her.

I told Mireya from the beginning I had no intention of *adjusting.* To me that sounded far too close to giving in, giving up. I'd make whatever accommodations I needed to, but I wasn't going to subject myself to some hokey spiritual journey meant to help me embrace my inner wolf. That was for damned sure.

But then the nightmares began. I started to lose time around the full moon. I couldn't control my beast, couldn't control the change. The straw that broke the proverbial camel's back? Waking up one morning, miles from campus in Cameron Park. I'd changed back right in front of a vagrant. He'd been drinking something wrapped in a brown paper sack. When I stood and approached him, he tossed the bag aside, fell to his knees and started to pray, head bowed, eyes closed. After spending several minutes begging the good Lord for forgiveness and promising never to drink again, he found me still standing there, naked as the day I was born. It didn't take much to convince him to let me borrow his extra pair of pants. They had been too short and filthy dirty. But beggars couldn't be choosers and I didn't have a whole lot of options. Truth be told? I still didn't.

That's why I was here, spending my spring break on "retreat". The incident had convinced me Mireya was right. I needed to strengthen my psychic connection to the pack and practice volitional transformation. If I didn't get myself under better control, something bad was going to happen.

My father was under the impression I'd gone snowboarding with my buddy Travis. Travis thought he was acting as my alibi so that I could sneak off with a girlfriend my father didn't exactly approve of. There was no girlfriend. And if I were to be honest with myself, I would admit there were few friends these days I was comfortable around, including Travis. I guess you can't be at peace when you're living a lie.

"Did you hear that?" Mireya asked. She'd come to a stop and I realized it too late. I was still running at full speed and

slammed into her, hard. We rolled in the snow, clods of it adhering to the thick fur of our coats.

"Jesus, Jake!"

I'd landed on top of her. In human form she was about five feet tall. I was over six. She was strong as a wolf and fast, but she was smaller than I was.

"You all right?"

"Yeah." She tried to shake it off.

Ryan caught up with us, his concern for her evident. *"You're limping, can you make it back?"*

"You let the doe get away!" Wright complained.

"I'm fine, Wright," Mireya said. *"Thanks for asking."*

Ryan dipped his head, padded over to Mireya and leaned down to lick her front right paw.

"Really," she assured him, turning away shyly. *"I'm fine."*

Then I heard it. A growl of frustration.

Mireya's head picked up. *"Did you catch it that time?"*

"Yeah. Sounds human." I scented the air. *"Smells human."*

"Check it out," she said. *"Ryan and I will catch up."*

I didn't need to be told twice. I took off at a run across the clearing, stopping at the side of a steep embankment. There were a few trees along the edge and several young saplings. A series of footprints in the snow led right up to the rim.

"Someone down there?" Wright asked. He was just a pup, only thirteen. Wright had been born normal, but had the misfortune of having a mother who was addicted to dangerous drugs and even more dangerous men.

She let one of those men into her home. He beat them. Turned them. Then when he tired of them, he abandoned them.

That was six months ago. Now his mother was God knows where and Wright lived here on the ranch. The sheriff drove him out one morning and handed him over to Dakota, our Alpha, no questions asked. And Dakota took him in, no questions asked.

I inched forward slowly, stretched out on my stomach, my hind legs spread out behind me. A section of the ground had obviously given way once.

"Stay back," I told Wright just as I reached the lip of the crevasse and peered down.

There was a woman. The instant her deep brown eyes connected with mine I smelled her fear. I knew what she was thinking, I'd been there before and it wasn't too long ago.

It was a bad climbing accident. I had been knocked unconscious and banged up pretty bad. By the time I came to, night had fallen and the wolves had gathered around me. At first I thought they were going to attack me. They didn't. They weren't normal wolves. Together, they dragged me to safety.

I still remembered the gleam of their teeth in the moonlight as they bit down, grabbing onto my clothing, being careful not to tear into it until... It was just one little graze on my forearm. The pack may have rescued me, but they took my life. Part of me would always hate them for that.

"N-nice doggie," the woman said softly, her teeth chattering in the cold.

There was a stream below her and it looked like she'd landed in it when she fell. She wore blue jeans, a navy wool pea coat and a cream-colored knit cap. The jeans were soaked through.

"What's—"

It was Ryan. He and Mireya had caught up to me.

"Stay there!" I growled. *"Don't touch her. Don't..."*

"We can't leave her down there," Wright protested.

"Jake." Ryan stepped closer.

I pushed back from the edge, fury raging through me. I snarled and attacked, my lips curled back, my teeth bared. I latched on to his throat, my jaw clamped down.

"Jake!" Mireya called.

I had Ryan pinned.

"Jake!"

Mireya jumped on me. She was more powerful than she looked and sank her teeth into my right ear.

"Back off," she growled.

I'm not sure how I managed to do it, but I released my hold on Ryan and threw her off. She landed with a yelp just a few feet away on the hard pack of the snow.

"Don't touch her," I repeated, my eyes still on Ryan.

"I-I won't," he promised, his eyes darting anxiously over to Mireya. *"I swear. Mireya? You okay?"*

I looked at Mireya, then lowered my head in submission. She was pissed and I couldn't blame her. *"I can save her. I can run back, revert to human form and return with the necessary gear. The trip shouldn't take me much more than an hour."*

"What if she doesn't last an hour?" Ryan asked. *"We have no idea how long she's been down there."*

"She'll last," I snapped, not wanting to even entertain the possibility she wouldn't. *"You just stay up here and watch her."*

"You don't give anyone orders," Mireya reminded me. *"You haven't earned the right."*

We didn't have time for this bullshit.

"What are we gonna do, let the girl die while we fight over hierarchy? You and I both know I don't give a flying fuck about that. I can save her and not like you saved me. I can really save her, Mireya. Let me do this."

There was a long, pregnant pause.

Ryan stepped forward. *"If I haven't said it before, I'm sorry, Jake."* He brushed softly against me, ears back, tail low. Then he glanced up at Mireya. *"What do you say?"*

Almost any other time his apology would have been welcome. Even if it hadn't been intentional, it was his fault I was a werewolf. Ryan had been the one to turn me. He was my maker.

"Go," Mireya agreed. *"Go!"*

I took off with a purpose I hadn't felt in ages. Until now, I'd been convinced they should have left me to die. Until now, I'd had nothing but resentment for the fact they hadn't. I'd spent weeks in denial, waiting for that first full moon to hit, then months after in abject misery. I kept searching my soul, looking for a reason, any reason, to justify why it had happened...and here it was. Here *she* was.

Each and every time my feet hit the ground, pain jolted through my legs. My arches burned and throbbed. My feet were cold and wet, even with the second pair of socks I'd quickly thrown on. The black Luccheses I was so fond of hadn't been designed for running, but despite the blister forming on the back of my left heel, I knew they were serving me better than my running shoes would have.

"How close are you?" Mireya asked.

The intrusion surprised me. It came as I was leaping over a fallen tree. I faltered on the landing and ended up sprawled in the snow.

"Jake?"

"Here." Climbing to my feet, I dusted the snow off my jeans and continued. *"I'm almost at the clearing."*

"Okay." Mireya sighed and the sound left me with a sense of foreboding.

"What's wrong?"

"She's not shivering as much. Things don't look good, Jake. You need to hurry. She's entering stage two hypothermia. She—"

Mireya stopped when I burst through the clearing. As I got closer I saw Ryan and Wright there with her, waiting and watching.

"She just nodded off," Ryan reported. *"Do you need me to help?"*

"Thanks, I've got it."

I unfastened the backpack I had been carrying, dropping it on the snow at my feet. Within seconds the equipment I had grabbed from the shed back at the ranch was out and the rescue rope was securely anchored to a tree. With practiced ease I slipped into the chest harness and seat harness, adjusting the leg loops and cinching everything down securely. Then I quickly attached the extra biners, webbing, ascenders, a Prusik, and finally, the second harness.

"What's the plan?"

"Gonna repel down, bring the lady up," I told Mireya before turning to approach the edge.

She grabbed hold of the bottom of my jeans with her teeth and stopped me. *"What if you can't do it by yourself? If she's unconscious and you can't wake her, it will be a dead lift."*

"I can do this," I assured her. *"I'm strong and I'm an experienced climber."*

"That area isn't stable," she argued.

"Let him try, Mireya," Ryan said. *"Please?"*

She finally let go with a growl. *"Be careful."*

I nodded and eased down onto the ground, sliding back gingerly on my stomach until finally I slipped over the edge of the precipice. When I'd checked earlier, the drop looked to be about thirty feet. I'd repelled down steeper and deeper faces before. The first time I went climbing with my father and older brother I was seven. We'd gone on dozens and dozens of trips since. I'd even done rescue drills similar to this one, but they'd never been real and never in the snow. I proceeded with caution.

The blizzard was in full force now. Even with my enhanced vision I couldn't see the bottom of the ravine. I descended as quickly as I could, landing just a few feet from the woman. I saw where she had started to dig out a trench in the side of the hill, presumably to protect herself from the elements before succumbing. Her body was covered in snow, her lips tinged blue. I looked up, but the snow was coming down even heavier. Visibility was down to just a few feet.

"What's happening?" Mireya asked.

I fell to my knees alongside the woman. She was beautiful. My insides shook with fear as I ripped off my gloves and dropped them beside her. I said a silent prayer that I wasn't too late, then I checked her pulse. She had one. It was strong and steady. She was alive. For now. It was up to me to make sure she stayed that way.

I stood and removed the extra harness.

"Looks like you could use a lift, darlin'," I shouted over the din of the wind.

Her eyes fluttered open, her lids seemed heavy, her gaze glassy as she stared at the tips of my boots. I knelt and lifted her, cradling her in my arms.

"You with me, sweetheart?"

Snowflakes were clinging to the tips of her lashes. She smiled weakly.

"I'm with you, cowboy," she whispered, her voice tremulous and a little hoarse. "Where in the world did you come from?"

"Originally? Dallas." I brushed off the dusting of fresh powder that had accumulated on her face. The flesh underneath was red from the cold.

"What the fuck is going on?" Mireya demanded.

She was afraid. Mireya wasn't prone to cussing.

"I've got her. I'm going to start the ascent in a minute. Once I'm close to the top I'll let you know, so you can take off and go ahead. I'm gonna bring her back to the ranch."

"She probably needs to go to a hospital, Jake."

"Look around you, Mireya. The roads are going to be closing if they aren't closed already. Until someone plows us out, we're probably going to be stuck."

"Once you give the signal we'll go on ahead," she relented. *"I'll explain to Dakota. As soon as the woman's recuperated, she leaves. Agreed? You have work to do, Jake. You aren't here to play nursemaid...or doctor."*

"I remember why I'm here."

"How did you find me?"

Since I was a terrible liar I stuck as close to the truth as possible. "I was just a little ways back in the clearing when you cried out. I would have been here sooner but I had to run back to my cabin for equipment. Can you stand, sweetheart?"

"Allison."

I smiled. "Can you stand, Allison?"

"I think so." She nodded and, moving onto her knees, faced me. "What's the plan?"

No nonsense. I liked that. I put my gloves back on, stood and offered her my hand. She took it and let me pull her up. She was a little unsteady at first and I was hesitant to let go.

"Depends on what kind of condition you're in."

"Just tell me what to do." The determination in her voice was encouraging.

"First we get you strapped into this harness. Do you know how to climb?"

She shielded her eyes with one mitten-covered hand and looked up at the face of steep snow. "I've never climbed anything like this."

A strong gust of wind blew through the passage. Allison stumbled. She bumped into me and I had to wrap my arms around her in order to prevent her from falling.

"Shit! Sorry."

"It's all right," I assured her. "I've got you."

"I'm not usually so... I don't know what's wrong."

"The less time we spend out here the better. The storm's getting worse and the wind chill is picking up." I unclipped the spare harness. "I'm gonna help you into this. Hold on to me, all right? Can you manage?"

She nodded.

It was slow going and awkward, but we did it.

"Now what, Dallas?" she asked as I cinched down the last strap.

I paused to retrieve the two bottles of water from my backpack. I opened the first one and handed it to her.

"I'm going to use this webbing and the biners to connect our harnesses. Then I'm going to haul us out of here as fast as I can. Drink some water."

"My car's miles away, six or seven. I don't think I can make it back that far. I can't believe I was so stupid. When I started out this morning the sky was clear. I..."

She glanced down at the bottle. Her hands were shaking. When she looked back up her eyes connected with mine. They were filled with tears.

"It's going to be all right. Don't be hard on yourself. The storm blew in from nowhere. The ranch where I'm staying, it's closer." I opened the second bottle of water and swallowed down half the contents before realizing she'd yet to take a sip. "Drink. You need the water."

"How far is it?"

"A few miles."

She looked up. The top of the ledge was invisible, there was no way for her to judge the distance. "So all we have to do is get back up there, then walk a few miles."

"All you have to do is hold on to me, darlin'," I said, trying to make what we were about to do sound simple. I finished attaching her harness to mine. "Just hold on."

We were in position now and ready to make our ascent. I'd done this before with packs as heavy as Allison was. I was younger then, weaker, still human. For the first time, I was grateful for my wolf. It was with me and would get us through this.

"I'm just going to slow you down, Dallas."

"The name is Jake and," I reached up for the rope, "I've always liked it slow."

Chapter Two

"How close are you, buddy?" Ryan asked.

"I've got about half a mile to go." I told him. *"It took me almost two miles to convince her to let me carry her."*

"Stubborn?"

"Like you wouldn't believe. I finally had to just lay it on the line and tell her she was being ridiculous. Her pride was slowing us both down."

"How'd that go over?"

"I'm carrying her, aren't I?"

"I gotta hand it to you, Jake. You have an enviable way with women."

"You got a fire going?"

"The fire's started, your bed is turned down, we put a case of bottled water on the counter, and there's a kettle of stew on the stove. I just made the last trip to your cabin to drop off cornbread and an extra blanket. Mireya says you need to get the woman's body temperature back up and hydrate her."

"Me? My cabin? Mireya's the nurse."

"Her leg was injured worse than she was letting on and she put more strain on it running back here. She couldn't make the last half-mile."

I inwardly winced. The injury was my fault.

"Tell her I'm sorry."

"Tell her yourself later. I'm going back for her now, just as soon as I gather up some warm clothes. We'll walk back. This one's up to you, Jake. Dakota thinks it'll do you good to think of someone other than yourself."

"You've got to be fucking kidding me!"

"Nope."

"Dakota!"

"He's not going to answer you," Ryan said. *"Anything you need, anything you want, you need to go through me."*

"You?"

"Yup."

"I don't understand. You're Omega."

"Yeah, but at least I'm pack."

"And I'm?"

"According to Dakota, you're still trying to make up your mind."

"What's that mean?"

"We'll talk later. For now, focus on the girl. You saved her, buddy. You did it. Dakota says from here on out, she's your responsibility."

The cabin I'd been assigned was on the edge of the compound. It was furthest from the main ranch house where common meals were served and where Dakota lived. Pine Ridge Ranch was kind of a resort, a place where tourists came to ride horses, hike trails, and sing songs together around the campfire. All of the members of our little pack both lived and worked at Pine Ridge, or nearby in town. I was the only exception.

"You saved me," I reminded Ryan just as I reached for the cabin door. *"So I'm your responsibility?"*

"Yup. You need me, call."

"We're here," I told Allison as I stepped up onto the porch, stomping to knock the snow off my boots. I turned, extended the arm situated under her knees, then grasped the doorknob and twisted.

The instant I pushed through and crossed the threshold I smelled the stew. The transformation itself burns an inordinate amount of calories. The additional exertion had left me absolutely ravenous. But the need to eat would have to wait.

The cabin was small, with only the one room in addition to the bathroom. The knotty pine interior was rustic but inviting. There was a fireplace in one corner with a queen-size four-poster bed in front of it. At the foot of the bed was a pine chest. The only other furnishings were the two chairs and a small, rectangular table.

I laid Allison down on the braided rug in front of the fire and quickly pulled off my gloves. First I removed her boots and socks, then her mittens. "We need to get your body temperature up." I slid one arm under her shoulders to lift her slightly and with my free hand I began to unbutton her coat. I'd put the fire out before we'd left. Several hours had passed since then and despite Ryan's restarting it, the cabin was still frigid.

She pushed my hands away. "I can do it." Her breath froze on the air.

I stood, shed my own coat and dropped it in front of the door. "You're soaked through," I pointed out, before sitting down on the chest. "The back of your coat and your jeans are both wet."

"When I fell I rolled into the river." Her teeth were chattering, her fingers trying to work the buttons on her coat.

I tugged off my boots. "Shit!" I winced. My feet were killing me and the boots hadn't come off easily. There was some blood on the outside of one big toe and both heels.

"You're hurt." She was still fumbling to release the coat buttons.

I yanked my sweatshirt over my head and ran it over my wet hair. "I'll be fine. I heal fast."

"Christ, it's cold in here!"

I was bare-chested and barely noticing. My body temperature seemed to run hot these days.

I dropped my sweatshirt at the foot of the hearth, then reached for the fire poker and turned over the logs, exposing the bright orange underside, stoking the fire.

"God damn it!" she growled. "My fingers aren't working."

"Come here." I offered her my hand and pulled her to her feet.

"Jake—"

Before she was able to finish her sentence I'd taken the coat off her and had begun to work on removing the sweater.

"Arms up."

I lifted the sweater over her head and her cap came off at the same time, releasing a spill of soft, chestnut waves. The simple white cotton camisole she'd been wearing came off too, leaving her breasts bare and exposed.

My gaze fixed on her, on her beautiful, deep brown eyes, silken hair, full lips and those fantastic tits.

Allison gasped, reaching for the sweater with one hand while she tried to cover herself with the other.

I politely averted my gaze, but not before the image emblazoned itself on my mind. Perfect pink nipples, hardened and peaked, jutting out from glorious mounds. My cock hardened. It had been a tragically long time since I'd been with a woman.

"Let me finish undressing you. Then you can get under the covers," I told her, trying to ignore the way she looked, the way she smelled.

"Yeah, right, Dallas. Give me back my sweater." She snatched the quilt off the end of the bed and shielded herself with it. "I should warn you, my mother forced me to take years of karate."

"Your mother?"

"She warned me about guys like you."

I tossed the sweater and camisole onto the floor before sliding my hands beneath the blanket and reaching for the top button of her jeans, quickly unfastening it.

"Nah, she was warning you about those other guys. Your mamma would love me." I placed my hands on her hips, turned her around and lowered the zipper. "Hold on to the bedpost."

Allison had a small waist and a fine ass that filled her jeans out nicely.

"You're shaking like a leaf," I observed.

She glanced back at me over her shoulder. Her eyes dropped to the floor demurely. "I could have died out there, Jake."

"But you didn't." I wondered for the first time if she might be going into shock.

The jeans were wet and the bottom half was crusted with snow from our trek. They weren't budging. I reached for the hunting knife I'd left on the mantel above the fireplace, cut a two-inch slice in the waistband, then grabbed hold of each side and ripped, revealing a deliciously sinful pair of black lace panties.

I crouched behind her and tugged down the heavy, soaked-through fabric until it was bunched around her ankles, and I helped her step out of it. Covered only in the sheer lace and the rich scent of arousal, she was positively mouthwatering. I closed my eyes to steady myself.

"Go on, the bed will be warm."

I meant to pull back, to pull away, honest I did, but despite my command she hadn't moved—not one inch. I swallowed. My throat had become dry. Underneath the notes of citrus and pine, underneath the smell of wet snow and her sweet sex, she smelled like me, she smelled like pack, like home. It was temporary, from holding her, and already it was fading. The wolf in me didn't want it to fade. It wanted to cover her, to rub up against her, to mark her as his.

"I don't normally have to ask a woman more than once to get into my bed."

I tossed the jeans behind me and stood, my hands ghosting up the length of her body while I imagined the feel of its softness with longing.

"I'm going." Allison turned and moved slowly to the bed, saying nothing. She climbed onto it and slipped between the clean, white sheets.

"I'll get an extra blanket..."

"Could you..."

"Could I what?"

She lay on her side, her back to me, the covers up to her neck. She might have been crying. I wasn't sure and it didn't seem right to ask, not if she was trying to hide it.

"Would you mind holding me?"

I glanced down at the snow-encrusted bottom of my jeans. Soon they'd be sopping wet. I shucked them off before sliding into bed and shifting over toward her, spooning up against her until my body was molded to hers.

"Better?"

"Not yet, but I will be, eventually."

I pulled her flush to me, close enough that my erection pressed into her backside.

Her entire body tightened, whether from fear or excited anticipation, I wasn't sure. I decided it would be best to address the awkwardness of the moment head on.

"I'm sorry, my body's reacting to yours. Don't worry. I know what this is and what it isn't."

"And what is this?"

"This is just about my body warming yours. In another minute or two, you'll stop shaking. Then I'll stoke the fire and make you some hot chocolate."

"I don't need hot chocolate." She moved and her leg slid over mine. It was silky smooth. I imagined the feel of it wrapped around my waist. Unable to resist, I placed my hand on her hip.

"What is it you need, Allison?"

She turned to face me. "I don't know."

"Yes, you do. Tell me."

She shook her head. "I used to know. It seems I've...lost track of that somehow. I used to be so sure of things, so confident. When there was something I wanted, I'd just reach out with both hands and grab it. You know what I mean?"

I reached behind her neck with one hand, tilted her head up, and looked deep into her eyes. I understood losing track of what I needed, what I wanted. I used to be sure of everything. Lately I hadn't been sure of anything. "I know exactly what you mean."

"Do you?"

"Yes."

Her lips were now dangerously close. They were full and lush and mine for the taking. But I knew taking them now, taking her now, would be a mistake. Something had started to build between us and whatever it was, it was compelling and it was about more than sex.

"Tell me."

"I want to kiss you, badly."

"Yet you're holding back."

I rolled onto my back and stared up at the ceiling. "It would be a mistake."

"A mistake?"

"It's not what you want, what you need."

"Is this real? Are you real?"

I turned my head and looked at her. My heart clenched. "What do you mean?"

Allison leaned up on one elbow. "Maybe I'm hallucinating. Maybe I'm still at the bottom of the ravine."

I gathered her into my arms, pulled her half on top of me. "You're not. You're here, safe. I promise." Her head was resting comfortably on my chest, her hand splayed out over my stomach. "Besides, if you were going to fabricate some knight in shining armor to rescue you, surely you would have done better than me." I ran my fingers through her hair. It was thick, but soft, like dark brown velvet. "In case you haven't noticed, I'm a little rough around the edges."

Allison sighed. "Some girls like it rough...around the edges."

True. Not her though. I'd bet my life on it. There was a quietness about her, a stillness. But there was darkness too. And depth. Like the calmness of a lake on a warm summer night, she called to me. Lord help me, I wanted to dive right in. "You strike me as a woman who prefers her men polished."

She lifted her head and looked me in the eye. "Maybe that was true once. Now I'd rather have the cold, hard truth."

She rolled off and pulled away. She was once again in her original position, facing the wall. Perhaps she thought she'd revealed too much.

"Spoken like a woman who's been badly burned," I said.

"Let's just say I have baggage."

"We all have baggage." I lightly traced the length of her spine with my index finger "Someone hurt you, badly."

"My once-upon-a-time didn't end happily-ever-after." Her tone was wistful. "Let's just leave it at that."

Apparently the past was off limits, at least for now.

"Rest. You're tired. When you wake up, we can eat." I started to shift away.

"Don't go."

I froze, waiting for her to say more. She didn't. After a minute I moved closer, testing the waters.

"Is this okay?" I whispered into the silence of the room, gingerly placing my hand on her waist.

She nodded, taking my hand and threading her fingers through mine. "It's more than okay." Then she settled back into the circle of my arms and drifted off.

Chapter Three

I was running through the forest. The snow was so cold and coming down so heavy it felt as if I was being rained on by glass, thin shards pelting against my naked skin. But I couldn't stop. I couldn't slow down. If I did, it would find me. It would be all over. I lengthened my stride, pushing myself like never before. I could outrun this, whatever it was. I could get away. Escape. If only I could push through the pain.

The clearing was up ahead, covered in a blanket of white. Unspoiled. Pristine. My lungs burned, the cold air scalding them, scorching them. Then I felt it, the brush of fur rolling, unfurling. Faster. Faster, I pushed myself. Jumping over fallen trees. Ducking under branches. Trying to avoid the rocks buried beneath the snow. My feet were cut and bleeding.

As I reached the edge of the clearing I saw them. Wolves. They weren't chasing me. They were waiting for me—baying, calling.

"God, no!" I shouted out, raising my arms up to the sky. Begging. Pleading. I threw my head back and searched the heavens, realizing too late, and only then, as I stared into the light of the full moon, that the beast I'd been running from was *me*.

"It's easier if you don't fight it," one said.

"Just let go," another said. *"Let it happen."*

"Accept what you are."

But I couldn't. I didn't. I fought. I fought to hold on as my bones broke and knitted back together, muscle and sinew tore apart, reshaped, then reformed. My screams shattered the darkness, merging with the sounds of the wolves until they were indistinguishable. Claws formed, teeth elongated and finally, when I was no longer able to stand on my own two feet, my flesh shredded in an explosion and a thick coat of fur burst forth, allowing me to blend into the shadows.

My eyes flew open.

Night had fallen and my breaths were coming quick and heavy. I was drenched in sweat despite the fact that the fire was almost out and the temperature inside the cabin had dropped.

I climbed out of bed and moved quietly over to the window. The snow continued to fall outside. The moon had risen, and predictably, I with it. I was always more alive, more aware when the moon was up, as if its light was a source of energy. Its power radiated through me, making each and every nerve hum in an inexplicable way.

"Are you okay?"

I closed my eyes and nodded. "Bad dream." I wiped the sweat from my brow with my forearm.

"Is it still snowing out?"

"Yes." I walked over to the stove and lit the flame under the stew. "We need more wood, we're almost out." I found my duffle bag and dropped it on top of the bed. "I won't be long."

I pulled a T-shirt out of the bag and slipped it over my head. Then I picked up the jeans I'd been wearing earlier, put them on and zipped them up. They were still wet around the bottom, but they would do.

"Are my clothes dry?"

I looked at Allison, really looked at her. She was sitting up in bed. She had the covers clutched to cover her breasts, but I could clearly see the line of her back and the curve of her buttocks. She was bathed in moonlight, her skin glowing with its iridescence, her hair tousled from sleep. The image took my breath away.

"Jake?"

"I'm thinking of telling you they aren't, even if they are."

"You'd lie to me?"

I pulled my running shoes out of the duffle and flashed her a lopsided grin. "Obviously not." I dropped the shoes onto the bed, then feigned lifting up the edge of the covers. "Seems you've rendered me powerless. You don't have any kryptonite in there, do you?"

"No!" she laughed, batting at my hand. "If I had any kryptonite on me, you would know it. You're a snuggler, Dallas."

I sat down on the edge of the bed and slipped on the runners. "I wasn't *snuggling*. I was just trying to keep your skinny ass warm, darlin'."

She flopped back down and stretched luxuriously. "A man who doesn't lie and thinks I have a skinny ass. I'm more convinced than ever I've died and gone to heaven."

I leaned across the bed and brushed an errant strand of hair out of her eyes. "I bet he's one sorry bastard."

Confusion marred her brow. "Who?"

"The guy who lost you."

Allison turned her head to the side. "I don't think he's sorry at all," she murmured, giving me a peek of her past.

"So he's a stupid bastard," I said before climbing to my feet and grabbing my coat.

She looked back and smiled.

"I'll be right back. The stew will be hot soon." I headed for the door. "Don't know about you, but I'm starving."

Chapter Four

When I returned to the cabin Allison was standing in front of the stove, wearing the only dress shirt I'd brought with me.

"The stew has a way to go yet before it's hot."

"It sure smells good, though. And that shirt looks far better on you than it does on me," I said as I kicked the door shut, my arms filled with a half a dozen logs. I dropped them into the wood basket next to the hearth, then pulled my gloves off.

She turned around. "You don't mind?" she asked, rubbing one long, lithe leg against the other, just like a cricket.

Christ, she was sexy.

I tossed one of the logs onto the grate, added some tinder and stirred the ashes below, blowing on them gently until the fire caught.

"Honestly? I would have preferred you stay naked and in my bed." I toed off my runners and placed them on the hearth where the heat would dry them out. I unbuttoned, unzipped, and just as I was about to pull down my pants I looked up.

Allison averted her gaze while I stripped. I hung the jeans over the back of one of the chairs, the wet legs close to the fire. Then I slipped on a pair of sweatpants and walked over to her. "But barefoot, half naked and in the kitchen works for me too."

I snaked one hand around her waist and casually pulled her against me, wanting her to feel the effect she had on me. I glanced over her shoulder into the pot of stew. "It's starting to warm up."

"Yeah." She sighed, pushing back ever so slightly, applying pressure that was amazing, yet torturous. "You said you were hungry."

"If I remember correctly, I used the word starving, and I am." I swept her hair over one shoulder baring her neck.

She could have pulled away. Instead she leaned her head to the side, it was a clear invitation. "It should be ready any minute."

I leaned down and whispered in her ear, "I'm ready now and craving something other than the stew."

"I thought you liked it slow, Dallas."

"I do." My mouth was close enough to her neck I knew she could feel every pulse of my breath.

"Seems like you're moving awfully fast."

The act of sleeping together, my body wrapped around hers, had felt so intimate. But it had only served to whet my appetite. It seemed that was true for her too. She may have been expressing some doubt, but her body wanted mine, and that certainty couldn't be denied. I could smell her arousal and it was driving me crazy.

"Darlin', I haven't even begun to move. Trust me, when I do, you'll know it."

"Jake—"

"I didn't want to take advantage before. You were tired, vulnerable. If I'm misreading the signals, if you want me to stop, just say the word." I moved one hand to her breast and gave it a gentle squeeze. "Do you want me to stop?" I asked, my voice rough with want.

"No. No, I don't want you to stop."

She turned to face me. That's when I noticed it—a gold chain dangling from her neck and on it a simple gold band. Her tits had distracted me earlier. I hadn't noticed the ring when I'd been undressing her, but I did now. It was a wedding ring.

"You're married." I released her.

It sounded like an accusation. I hadn't meant it to.

Allison shook her head, then she walked around me, moving closer to the fire. "Divorced. It...ended badly." She wrapped her arms around herself in what appeared to be a protective gesture.

I sat on the edge of the bed and waited, wondering if she was going to tell me more. She didn't.

"Last summer I worked on an especially gruesome divorce case. It just about killed me," I told her. "It was a mess. And the worst thing was they used the kids to get to one another. I swore off divorce law after that. It's not my cup of tea, watching people who used to be in love tearing one another down."

Allison walked over to me. Touching her seemed natural now, easy. I placed my hands on her waist and pulled her closer, spreading my knees to accommodate her.

"And what kind of law is your cup of tea?"

"Criminal law, prosecution."

"Keeping the world safe from bad guys by day and rescuing damsels in distress by night. You're a real hero, Dallas," she teased.

I reached behind me until I found the edge of the covers, then pulled them down and inched back. "A hero, huh?"

"Yeah."

"I probably deserve a reward of some kind. Don't you think?"

There was a pretty obvious tent forming in my sweats and her eyes drifted down to it.

Allison licked her lips.

"I'm not good at this. I'm out of practice," she murmured, almost to herself. Her cheeks flushed and she started to turn away, unable to look me in the eye.

"I can help with that," I offered, holding my hand out and encouraging her to climb onto the bed and straddle my hips. "Question is," I added, cupping the side of her face and gazing into those dark sable eyes, "how much help do you want?"

Allison smiled, then relaxed, placing her hands on my chest.

"How much you willing to give, Dallas?"

"Shucks, ma'am," I drawled, grinding myself into her pussy. "You ask me real nice, I'll give this all to you."

She looked past me, her expression clouded over with momentary indecision.

"You gonna be thinking about him?" I fingered the gold band hanging from the chain around her neck.

"Would it matter?"

"Yes," I admitted, much to my chagrin. "I guess I'm old fashioned that way."

"Gavin proposed to me on the bluff, right where the snow sheared off. This ring was supposed to be a symbol of his love and fidelity. In the end he gave me neither."

The sadness in her voice was almost palpable. I wanted to tell her I was sorry. Not sorry it ended, it probably needed to end, sorry for the pain and disappointment. But before I could say anything she shook off the mood, pulled back her shoulders, and continued.

"Jake, I came here intending to throw the ring down into the ravine. Right now, I can assure you, I'm not thinking about anyone but you."

I turned the necklace around until I could see the clasp. It was delicate with a small catch.

"Were you going to keep the necklace?"

"No."

I released the catch and the ring slid off the chain, onto the bed. Allison picked it up and placed it in my outstretched palm.

"As soon as the weather clears we'll go back there, together," I promised, reaching back to drop the necklace on the nightstand.

"And in the meantime?"

I slipped my hand around her neck and lowered her head toward mine before tracing the outline of her lips with the pad of my thumb.

"I'm going to kiss you."

The first one started tenuously, soft and slow, lips skimming over lips, uncertain. A little nibble, a flick of the tongue and she gasped, opening her mouth so I could slide inside.

I laced my hands through her long, thick tresses to pull her head closer, make the kiss deeper. I wanted to savor it, savor her. Allison's tongue responded as I stroked it, curling around mine, then pushing past my lips. She was taking what she wanted and I liked that.

She straddled my thighs, her palms flat on the mattress above my head, one on either side. My cock pressed into her taut stomach. She shifted slightly, her pussy grinding against my hipbone. I felt her dampness and the anticipation of sinking inside it, inside her, was almost my undoing.

Allison broke off the kiss, breathing heavily, her tits rising and falling in time with each exhalation.

"I want to feel you, skin on skin," I told her, reaching down with both hands.

"Don't—"

She wasn't quick enough. I tore through the lace panties, ripping them to shreds.

"Jake! Those were almost forty dollars!"

I lifted her off me and in one fluid motion I changed our positions. I wanted on top. I pulled the T-shirt over my head and stripped off my sweats.

"They were in my way." I hooked one hand underneath her knee and lifted her leg, opening her up nice and wide. As soon as I did, the tip of my cock found its target, velvety smooth and dripping with desire.

Before becoming a werewolf I would never have even considered having unprotected sex. Now, disease wasn't an issue. I couldn't catch a thing. Not even a common cold. And, another strange side effect, I'm only fertile for a couple months in the winter. The rest of the year I can get it up just fine, but I'm shooting blanks.

"God, I want you," I groaned, silently rejoicing in the fact that despite the snowfall outside, this was spring.

"Wait!"

"Wait?"

"Couples who are about to..." She seemed to be searching for the right word.

"Fuck?" I interjected helpfully.

She frowned. "Have sex."

That made me smile.

"Say fuck," I begged, letting the head of my dick slide up and down the length of her slick slit. "If you can't say it, I'm not sure you should be doing it."

"We shouldn't be doing this without a condom."

One of the few silver linings in this miserable cloud called lycanthropy and I wasn't going to be able to take advantage of it. Just as I was contemplating the unpleasantness of stuffing perhaps the biggest hard-on I'd ever had in my life back into my sodden jeans and setting out in the middle of the worst blizzard I'd ever seen in search of what was fast becoming the Holy Grail, Allison continued.

"I was tested, right after I found out Gavin was cheating on me. He said he'd always used protection. But he'd lied about so many other things..."

"And?"

"I'm clean, Jake. I haven't been with anyone since him and I'm on birth control."

I leaned down and kissed her then, softly on the mouth. "I've never had unprotected sex," I confessed quietly.

"Not once?"

"Not once. Trust me?"

I searched her eyes, looking for a response, waiting for a reply. Seconds ticked by.

"We don't have—"

"Shh." She placed her fingers over my mouth, silencing me. Allison's feet traced a path up the outside of my calves, my knees, my thighs. She wrapped her long, slender legs around my ass, pressing down, coaxing me in.

The head of my dick slid inside her. She was tight yet soft, her heat surrounded me. I resisted the urge to thrust into her. I'd teased her before about liking it slow, but right now my body craved it hard and fast and deep.

"Don't move." I bit down on my lip, fighting for control. "I swear if you move, this is going to be over embarrassingly fast. I don't want it to be over. God, you feel incredible."

"Listen to the wind," she murmured. "The storm is raging outside. We have lots of time. We can always do slow later."

I pulled out and leaned up. "Let me make you come first," I suggested, preparing to move down her body and fuck her with my mouth, my tongue.

She wouldn't have it and grabbed a handful of my hair to stop me.

"I want to feel you inside me." She wrapped her hand firmly around my cock, guiding it back to her entrance. "I'm ready." I was drowning in her wetness, slipping between the folds of her lips, past her clit, hard and ripe, sinking deeper and deeper until I was buried to the hilt, my balls touching her ass. Then I pushed in just a little bit more.

Allison gasped.

"You okay?"

"You're so deep."

"What do you want?"

"I want to feel alive."

I backed off a bit, then pushed in again, this time angling my hips so that the top of my dick would drag across her clit. In and out. Over and over.

"Christ!" she cried out.

I sensed it coming. The little telltale signs were all there, her breathing becoming more labored, the insides of her thighs quivering, the walls of her channel tightening, tensing in preparation.

"Squeeze me," I told her. "Bear down."

I held on to the headboard with one hand, my forearm extended to support my weight. Then I slid the other hand between us.

"Come for me." I circled her clit with the pad of my thumb. Allison arched up into my touch.

"Oh, God!"

The pace quickened. My stomach was a mass of coils, tightly wound and ready to explode.

"That's right." Her moans of encouragement spurred me on. Her hands wrapped around my biceps, nails digging in. I didn't care.

The wolf turned over inside me. There was a brush of fur; something was trying to fight its way through. I pushed it down.

"Roll over," I growled. "I want you on your knees."

I pulled out and turned her. Try as I might, I couldn't deny the beast's presence. It was there, inside me, pacing just below the surface. It had been too long, I wasn't sure I could control it. I couldn't afford to have her look into my eyes.

"Jake—"

I'd already wrapped my arm under her waist and lifted her onto her knees. "Shh." Covering her body with mine, I placed her hands on the headboard. "Hold on tight."

Her back was slick now with perspiration. My body glided against hers, my hips churning, the heat between us building.

"Come for me!" I demanded, finding her clit again and rolling it between my thumb and forefinger.

Allison cried out, the insides of her legs quivering. She was close, so close.

"That's it, baby." I arched, kissing her back. "Come with me. Come with me, darlin'."

And she did. She came with me.

And it was fucking fantastic.

Chapter Five

The cabin was toasty warm and I was sated in more ways than one. I'd feasted on the cornbread and chicken stew before turning my attention back to Allison. We'd spent the last few hours exploring one another's bodies and indulging in hot, sweaty sex. The kind I'd always dreamed of having. It was raw and uncomplicated. And I wanted more of it.

I rolled onto my side and studied Allison's back, resisting the urge to touch her. I listened intently to her breathing, trying to determine if she'd drifted off.

"What?" She'd been on the edge of sleep. Her voice sounded far away.

"You're amazing."

"I bet you say that to all the girls you save."

"Only the ones who swallow."

She pushed back against me. It was probably meant as a sign of reproach but my dick thought it encouraging. It was semi-hard and slipped right between the cleft of her ass.

"I should let you sleep," I murmured, gently kissing her shoulder.

"You should sleep too."

"Can't. Too many thoughts going through my head."

She rolled over, more awake now.

"What are you thinking about?" She ran the tips of her fingers across my forehead as if she were trying to smooth out the rough spots in my psyche. If that were her goal, she was going to need a hammer and a chisel.

"Doesn't matter, go to sleep."

She frowned.

"It's none of my business," I added.

"It's keeping you awake." She kissed me, softly on the mouth. "Ask."

"Tell me about your marriage, about your divorce. You said you had baggage. I want to understand."

"Why?"

"Because I like you. I want to see more of you."

She smiled. "I'm pretty sure you've already seen all there is of me, Dallas."

I threaded my fingers through her hair at the base of her skull and looked her in the eye, my gaze steady and unwavering. "I want to *see* you," I repeated.

She nodded and licked her lips. "You might not like everything you see."

"You haven't disappointed me yet."

She rolled over, gazed up at the ceiling, and sighed. "Suddenly I feel like I could use a drink."

"Water?"

"I was thinking more along the lines of scotch."

Every minute I was with this woman, I liked her more and more.

I climbed out of bed, walked over to the kitchen area, pulled a bottle of Johnny Walker Red Label out of one of the cupboards, and grabbed two glasses.

Allison sat up in bed. "You had scotch and you didn't use it to try to get me drunk and in the sack earlier?"

I made my way back over to her. "That wouldn't have been very honorable." After pouring each of us a generous glass, I set the bottle down on the floor.

"Do men still think of things like honor?"

I handed Allison her scotch, then crawled back into bed with the other. "Some do."

"Have you ever been in love, Dallas?"

"Can't say I have."

"You've never had your heart broken?"

"Superbowl Forty-Two When Eli Manning threw that thirteen-yard touchdown pass to Plaxico Burress with thirty-five seconds to go in the fourth quarter. I cried."

She frowned. Apparently she wasn't a football fan. Guess it's true, nobody's perfect.

"No." I continued, hoping I could make the frown disappear by giving her a real answer. "Not the way you mean. My mother died a couple years ago. That was hard. We were close. I miss her...still."

"I'm sorry." She reached for my hand and held it.

I shrugged. There wasn't really any more to say. I'd opened up and shared. Now there was nothing to do but bask in the small victory.

We lay next to one another for a bit, sipping scotch in companionable silence and looking out the window. The snow was still coming down, hard and heavy, and in the moonlight we could see it.

"When Gavin proposed, it was summer here," she began. "It was beautiful. Have you ever been here during the summer?"

"A few times."

"We'd met the year before."

Apparently, she was ready to talk about Gavin.

"How did you meet?"

"His practice offered one internship slot. It was quite coveted. I applied. I was thrilled when I was awarded the position. I hadn't thought the woman who'd interviewed me cared for me at all. It was only after we were married Gavin confirmed she hadn't. But it didn't matter. He'd watched the interview from behind a mirror and at the time he'd liked what he'd seen."

"Gavin's a..."

"Forensic psychologist. He makes a living assisting with jury selection, being an expert witness, that sort of thing. His practice was—is enormous."

"That's what you do too?"

"Not anymore." She took a sip of her scotch and swallowed. "Now I teach. I couldn't continue to work with him. Not after the break-up. I enjoy teaching. I enjoy standing on my own. Gavin casts a pretty big shadow."

"You're so full of light," I said, thinking out loud. "It's hard to imagine you living in anyone's shadow."

"When we met I was young and naïve. He was, as you said, polished. And confident. Oh, was he confident." She turned and studied me for a moment. "You're confident."

"About some things. Wouldn't say I'm polished though," I added, kicking back the remainder of my scotch, then smacking my lips together.

Allison laughed. "Anyway, things were good in the beginning."

"Until?"

She shrugged. "I grew up. The stars in my eyes faded. Gavin didn't love *me*. I don't think he's capable. What Gavin loved was that *I* was so in love with *him*."

"You deserve better."

She shook her head. "Dallas, how can you say that? You don't even know me."

"Anyone would have deserved better." I reached for the bottle, poured myself a bit more, and offered some to Allison.

"No thanks. I'm good."

"To love and be loved. It's what marriage is all about, right?"

"For most. At least in the beginning." Allison shifted onto her side. "If only it could stay that way."

"You want to know what my father said to me the day my mother died?"

"Yes."

"He said, 'Son, for over thirty years I've woken up every morning certain of one thing, I was about to fall in love with your mother all over again. What the hell am I gonna do tomorrow?'"

Her eyes misted over with tears. "What did you say?"

"I said, 'Let's go duck hunting'."

She gasped. "You shot at ducks? With guns?"

"No. We threw rocks at them. Of course we used guns."

"I was just about to accuse you of being romantic."

"You don't think a man can be a hunter *and* be romantic?" I climbed out of bed to throw another log on the fire.

That was the question, wasn't it? The one I had been struggling with on some level. How to reconcile the man and the beast, the civilized soul and the predatory animal.

"Maybe," she mused. "But could they be good at both? I don't know. Romance is about connecting. Hunting is about dominating, conquering—"

"Going in for the kill," I finished as I reached for the edge of the covers and pulled them off the bed, leaving Allison naked before me.

"Jake!" she yelped, folding one arm across her breasts, lowering her other protectively between her legs. Suddenly she was exposed, defenseless. Her pulse quickened. Her heart started to race. Her pupils dilated. It was intoxicatingly arousing.

"Allison," I said softly, grabbing hold of her ankles, separating her legs, and tugging. She slid another six inches down the bed.

She started to move, to protest, but then my eyes connected with hers and she froze in place. For several long moments I found myself wondering why, wondering what she'd seen in my gaze. Was it the beast or the man? Were they even separate any longer?

"Your move, Dallas."

I climbed slowly, steadily and with assurance up the length of her body, peppering kisses along the way, nuzzling into the hollow of her hipbone, nibbling, licking, breathing in deeply the musky smell of her sex, scenting traces of myself along the way. The canvas of her skin was already becoming familiar to me, familiar in a way that was comforting, soothing.

A sigh escaped her lips and she arched into me, her hips lifting slightly off the mattress.

"How about some more stew?" Resting my chin on the soft pillow of her stomach, I gazed up into her warm brown eyes.

"You've already had two helpings, you can't still be hungry."

"Are you kidding? I worked up quite an appetite. You're very demanding of your sex slaves."

"We should keep our strength up."

"Right. So, go fetch me some more stew, woman." I ordered, rolling off Allison so my back was to the wall. "Go on." I gave her a little nudge.

"*Fetch* you some more stew? You've got to be kidding. What about me?"

"Tell you what, you feed me now, I'll fuck you again later."

Allison's cheeks burned red.

"I can't believe you just said that."

"Believe it."

She rolled her eyes then slid from the warmth of the bed.

I smiled, feeling more content and satisfied than I had in months as I watched her pad, naked, across the floor and return with another steaming bowl.

The stew was delicious, fresh vegetables and big chunks of chicken in rich gravy. Allison and I ended up sharing it along with another slice of cornbread and more of the scotch.

We dined on a blanket in front of the fire and then, while the storm raged and wolves howled in the distance, we indulged in more hot, sweaty sex.

Allison's head rested on my chest, her arm encircled my waist, her left leg draped over mine.

"It'll be morning soon." I placed a gentle kiss on the top of her head. "Darlin'?"

"Hmm?"

"Come on." I slipped out from underneath her. "Get into bed."

"Can't," she protested. "My legs entirely stopped working three orgasms ago. Are you always this insatiable, Dallas?"

I leaned up on one elbow, rolled onto my side, and watched the play of firelight as it danced across her skin.

"Are you complaining?"

Allison smiled. "No."

"Good." I gave her fine round ass a playful swat before climbing to my feet. "You can stay another day, then." I started to gather up my clothes.

She rolled onto her back and gazed up at me, a glint of mischief in her eye.

"Another day?" She imitated my Texas drawl, dramatically batting her eyelashes. "Why, sir, whatever will we do?"

"I'm sure we can find some interesting ways to pass the time. You know, there are over sixty positions in the Kama Sutra." I stepped into my jeans and zipped them up.

"You've read the Kama Sutra?" Allison asked as she climbed to her knees.

"When I was twelve. I stumbled across a copy in the library. I was supposed to be doing a report on India."

She placed one hand on my abs, then reached up with the other, lightly grazing one of my pecs with her nails before teasing a nipple. "Do you remember chapter nine?"

"Can't say as I do, teacher. But I bet I'd find a refresher course...interesting."

"I guarantee you it will be far more interesting without your pants."

I was acutely aware of the fact I was hard again and that her mouth was just inches away from where I wanted it to be. I grasped her hands, pulled her to her feet, then threaded my hands through her hair and kissed her hard.

As our lips parted her knees buckled. Her exhaustion was apparent. A pang of guilt shot through me—I should have reined in my desire and better controlled my lust. Allison was right. I had been practically insatiable. I couldn't get enough of her. Was it because it had been such a long time? I hoped so.

Pushing aside the urge to apologize, I scooped her up and instead deposited her gently on the bed.

"Rest." I covered her with the blankets. "I won't be long."

"Where are you going?"

"I'm going to run over to the main ranch house. I want to see if they have news about the storm, maybe get some supplies. Got a hankering for anything special?"

"Just more of you."

"I won't be long. Shall I bring you back some coffee? Allison?"

There was no answer. She'd already drifted off.

Chapter Six

"Christ, it's a mess out there!" I stomped over to the stove in search of coffee. It was past breakfast time, but Ryan was addicted to the stuff and he almost always had a fresh pot brewing.

"Must you track snow all over my kitchen?"

Ryan was standing behind the large butcher-block table, kneading a loaf of bread. I poured myself a generous cup of the bitter brew, then blew across its steaming surface in order to cool it.

"You sound like an old woman." I took a sip.

"You reek of sex."

I set my cup down on the countertop, leaned casually against it and grinned.

"I reek of fantastic sex. Allison is amazing. And, while we're on the subject of sex, I have a few questions."

Ryan looked up at me, an uncharacteristic flash of anger evident in his eyes.

"I've got work to do. Go crow to somebody else."

"You know, maybe if you were getting some you wouldn't be so cranky."

"Maybe I'm saving myself," Ryan muttered, color rising in his cheeks. He hastily wiped his flour-covered hands across the front of his starched white apron.

"For what?"

"You wouldn't understand." Ryan sighed. "This human, she's not worthy of you."

"You haven't seen her ass," I replied.

Ryan smiled, and shook his head. "You're impossible. Go ahead, ask your questions."

"Allison said I was insatiable. She's right. It's suddenly as if I'm a walking hard-on. I figured it was because I hadn't been laid in months, but..."

"You're wondering if it's something else, something to do with the change."

"Yeah. I felt something I never felt before during sex. It seemed...dark. Like something was turning over inside me, pacing, caged."

"Your beast. It longs to escape, to break free."

"I can't let it. I need to control it."

"Control it?"

"Yeah."

But that was the rub, I wasn't sure I could. And, if I were to be totally honest with myself, I'd admit a small part of me wanted to know what it would be like not to.

Ryan shook his head and chuckled. "You think what you are, what I am, is an abomination against nature. We *are* nature, transcendent. The sooner you realize that, the sooner you'll realize your true potential. You're destined for greatness, Jake."

"Greatness, huh?" I took another sip of coffee.

"You don't believe me?"

"You'd look more credible without the apron."

Ryan ignored the good-natured jibe. "You're strong," he assured me. "Which is the biggest irony in all of this. Somehow,

I managed to make something better than me. You can learn to control your beast. Hell, you can learn to do more. You can harness its power. But you have to embrace it first. You have to stop running, stop wishing."

"Easy for you to say. You were born a lycanthrope. You haven't had to cope with losing everything."

"No," he sighed wearily before punching down the dough. "I've had to cope with accepting there are things I want which I'll never have."

"Horseshit. This is the U.S. of fuckin' A." I slapped him heartily on the back. "You can be whatever the hell you want."

"I'll never be Mireya's mate," he said, surprising the shit out of me.

For this I had to sit down.

"You want to marry Mireya?"

Ryan paused in his task and looked up at me, his sandy blond hair falling into his eyes.

"You have a lot to learn about being Were," he said softly.

"You gonna teach him?"

Samuel's enormous frame filled the doorway. The chiseled lines of his face hardened with disdain. I didn't usually feel small, but next to Samuel I did. His fist was bigger than my biceps. He was half Washoe. This morning his long black hair hung loose, spilling over his shoulders and midway down his back.

I turned toward Ryan, otherwise I might have noticed Samuel's intention sooner. By the time I realized he was coming for me it was too late. His right hand was around my throat, my back flat against the kitchen table. He had me pinned. The cup of coffee I'd been holding dropped to the floor and shattered.

"What the fuck?" I managed to choke out, reaching for his wrist.

"You think you're so tough?" Samuel growled, the bass rumble starting from someplace low in his belly and emanating up through his chest until his entire body hummed. "Flexing your muscles. Hoping to gain power, to move up."

"It wasn't like that, Samuel. I already told you, her injury was an accident," Ryan said, trying to sooth him. "He wasn't challenging Mireya."

It didn't do any good. Samuel had a point to make. "I want to be perfectly clear. If you think you can beat me, you are sorely mistaken. You're no competition, nothing but a pup. I can kick your ass with both hands tied behind my back. You need to be reminded of your place, boy."

"Samuel!"

I couldn't see her, but I recognized Mireya's voice.

Samuel released me instantly. My first instinct was to retaliate, but one look from Ryan told me that would be a mistake. Instead, I tried to say something conciliatory. "I have no intention of challenging anyone."

Mireya stepped between us. She was dressed for work in a pair of navy blue scrubs, her dark brown hair sensibly pulled back. "It's all right."

"How's the ankle?" I asked. Apparently it was the wrong thing to say. Suddenly the tension in the room was once again unbearably thick.

"Let me clean that up." Ryan nodded toward the broken pieces of crockery and spilled coffee on the floor.

Mireya stepped back and into Samuel's space. "Mind telling me what that was about?" The two of them were toe-to-toe. If she felt dwarfed by his size, she gave no indication of it. I had to admire her. The girl wasn't easily intimidated.

"What do you mean?"

"What do I mean?" she mocked, not buying the innocent act. "I'm only going to tell you this one more time. I can fight my own battles. I've tussled with bigger and badder than him. Hell, I've tussled with bigger and badder than you. I'm still here. What happened last night was an accident, pure and simple. Nothing more. Jake isn't a threat to me. He isn't a threat to you. Back off."

Samuel eyed me quietly for a few seconds before turning to Ryan. "The sheriff was here this morning. He followed the plow out to tell us there are a couple of guys missing."

"For how long?" Ryan asked.

"The distress call came in yesterday as the storm hit. They haven't heard anything since. Bastard finally admitted they need help. Dakota left with him about an hour ago. I'm gonna go lend a hand with the search. I don't want Dakota out there alone."

After depositing the remnants of the broken cup into the trash can, Ryan asked dutifully, "Need me to do anything?"

"If you can get into town later, pick Mireya up at the end of her shift," Samuel replied.

"There's no need. The way it's coming down the roads will be a mess by then. I doubt the plow makes it back," Mireya interjected. "I'll stay in town with one of the other nurses."

"The Sherriff promised us one more pass and Ryan was planning on stocking up on supplies anyway." Samuel fished a set of keys out of the front pocket of his blue jeans. "Take Wright with you. I don't want him out here all by himself."

"I'll be here," I reminded Samuel. He didn't seem impressed.

"Use my truck," he continued, tossing the keys to Ryan. "I'm taking Dakota's. After I drop Mireya off I'm going to meet him in town. Hopefully we can pick up the trail."

Ryan plucked the keys out of the air effortlessly. "Got it. I'll fix some sandwiches and coffee for you to take. Think you'll be back in time for super?"

"No way." Samuel glanced outside. "The guys were last seen heading up to High Camp. I'm hoping we make it to the station in Dalton's Pass by dark. If we haven't found them, we'll rest for a few hours then continue on."

"What about me?" I asked Samuel.

"What about you?"

"I'm an experienced climber. I could be of use to you out there."

"Boy, you've yet to convince me you're going to be of any use to us, period," Samuel said.

"Come on," I protested. "I want to help."

He handed me an apron and pointed to the sink full of dirty dishes behind me.

"You've got to be kidding."

Samuel turned his back on me and walked away. Mireya followed. He paused at the threshold of the door and let her pass through first. "When I get back," he said, "you and me, we're going to have ourselves a talk."

"Looking forward to it." I resisted the urge to flip him off.

Ryan and I watched as the truck pulled out of the long drive and headed down the road. "You know, if you didn't goad him so much, he wouldn't ride you as hard."

"I don't goad him."

Ryan removed his apron and tossed it onto the countertop. "I don't want you to take this the wrong way," he began, "but I think you should go."

"Where?"

"Away from here."

"Are you kidding? Mireya's been trying to convince me to come for months. Now I'm here and you want me to go?"

"It's not that I want you to go. It's…"

"It's what?"

"I'm afraid this pack is too small for you. If you stay, there's going to be trouble. Maybe a larger, more traditional pack—"

"It's not like I asked for this, Ryan."

"I know. It's not your fault. It's Dakota's. Ever since Rebecca died, he's been biding his time. He's not interested in leading or growing the pack, but he won't hand over the reigns to anyone else. With each passing year Samuel gets more and more bitter."

"Who's Rebecca?"

"Dakota's mate, Samuel's mother. She died about fifteen years ago."

"What happened?"

"I barely remember."

I didn't believe him and Ryan knew it.

"Ryan, I'm not going anywhere. I have no place else to go."

He looked out the window, a shadow of uncertainty passing across his features. He shoved his hands deep into his pockets. "When you have nothing it's safer. Because, then, you don't have anything to lose."

"Help me understand, Yoda."

Ryan turned and threw the dishtowel that had been draped over his shoulder at me. "You can be such an ass."

"I swear I wasn't this bad before the accident."

Ryan just shook his head.

"All right, I'm sorry. I'm listening. Talk to me."

"This wasn't always a tourist spot, you know. The pack was bigger once, much bigger. And much more powerful. We were happy."

"Until?"

"There was an all out war."

"Between packs?"

"Another pack moved into the area and attacked us without warning. There is nothing more dangerous than a rogue Alpha, a wolf who has lost respect for the traditions, who's forgotten the true meaning of pack, of knowing one's place, of right and wrong."

"Pack members were killed?"

Ryan nodded. "It was a savage bloodbath. Both my parents died, our Alpha was murdered along with his mate. Dakota watched as Rebecca went down. Something in him snapped, I guess. I've never seen..."

He swallowed hard. Then he turned away from me and resumed looking out the window.

"Samuel and I were the only other ones left. When the fighting started, Rebecca locked us in the root cellar. I was five. Samuel was eight. I'm not sure how we managed to get out. There are supposed to be rules. But there weren't any that day, only death."

"How many?"

"Twenty-five, maybe thirty. We found Dakota alive, but he was covered in blood, some of it his. He was hurt, badly, too badly to shift."

"Jesus. You and Samuel were just kids. What the hell did you do?"

"There's a lot about that time I don't remember. And I'm grateful for that. I suppose we did what we had to. We survived."

"This is more than your pack. Dakota and Samuel, they're like family to you."

"Exactly. For a long time it was just the three of us. About a year ago Mireya moved here."

"Where was she before?"

"Back east, some place in New England. She accepted a position at the hospital. She didn't have much money and called about renting one of the cabins. Samuel and Dakota were off hunting. I invited her out to the ranch so she could take a look. As soon as I laid eyes on her I knew..."

"She was a wolf?"

"She was *my* wolf."

"Your wolf?"

Ryan nodded solemnly.

"You're in love with her. Does she know?"

"Do you think I'm insane?"

"That's a rhetorical question, right?"

Ryan walked over to the kitchen sink, put the stopper in the drain, turned on the faucet full force, and donned a pair of bright yellow gloves. "Samuel and Mireya make sense. Mireya and I? We don't. Period. End of story."

He squeezed dishwashing soap into the sink and for a fleeting second I considered reminding him I was supposed to be doing the dishes. But then I have never been one to look a gift horse in the mouth.

"Is Samuel in love with Mireya?"

Ryan shook his head. "No, Samuel's not in love with Mireya. He's attracted to her because she's the strongest female."

"You're not even going to try to test the waters with her, see if she'd be interested?" I slipped the apron Samuel had thrown at me over my head and joined Ryan at the sink. "I'll dry."

59

"I know my place. Samuel is a born Beta. There's a good chance he'll be Alpha one day. Unless someone stronger comes along and takes the privilege away from him, that is. He's threatened by you."

"Mireya was right. Samuel doesn't need to worry about me. You, on the other hand..."

Ryan handed me a juice glass from breakfast and I began to dry it. "Jake, nobody goes from Omega to Alpha."

"I'm not talking about you becoming Alpha. Has it occurred to you maybe Mireya doesn't want an Alpha? She's smart, strong, sexy—"

"All women want Alphas."

"You've got a lot to learn about women."

"You think I really have a shot with her?"

"Absolutely! I'm telling you, man, you're a catch."

I placed the dry glass back on the shelf and lifted another from the drain board.

"You know. You'd look more credible without the apron."

"Says the man wearing bright yellow gloves to protect his hands while he does the dishes."

Ryan lifted one rubber encased hand out of the water and flipped me the bird.

"Nice," I said. "And to think, you want to kiss Mireya with that mouth."

"Not gonna happen."

"Grow a pair, for Christ's sake. Take a chance. What's the worst that could happen?"

"I'll be asked to leave?"

"Dakota wouldn't kick you out. He couldn't run this place without you."

Ryan turned off the water and removed his gloves. "He and Samuel have been going at it lately. Things are going to come to a head soon, I can feel it. Samuel's strong, he's always assumed he'd take over the pack. Until recently, keeping things small suited him, there was less competition."

"Then I came along?"

Ryan grabbed a clean cup out of one of the cupboards and poured himself a fresh cup of coffee. "Then you came along. Samuel's feeling the need to flex his muscles. He's itching for a fight, both man and beast. His wolf is still no match for Dakota."

I put away the last of the dishes. "But he figures he can kick my ass six ways from Sunday."

"Can he?"

I almost dropped the plate I was holding. "You think I can take Samuel? He's built like a line-backer."

"Maybe not today, but someday. You're power is growing. You're changing, evolving."

"Most days it feels like I'm devolving."

Ryan smiled. "So, tell me about Allison."

I spun one of the kitchen chairs around and sat, straddling the back of it. "I don't kiss and tell."

"Come on, let me live vicariously."

"She's smokin' hot. The chemistry between us is off the charts. I've never been with a woman like her." I hesitated for a minute. "She's older. More experienced."

It took Ryan a few extra seconds to swallow the sip of coffee he held in his mouth. "How much older?"

I shrugged. "I'm guessing she's in her early thirties. The age difference hasn't really come up and I'm not about to bring it up. It doesn't matter, anyway. What matters is that for whatever reason, we've really connected. I like her. A lot."

"What do you know about her?"

"She's from Southern California. Married. Divorced. She's a shrink and, get this, a college professor. Hey, you don't happen to have a short little plaid skirt I could borrow, do you?"

"No. I'm planning on wearing it tomorrow. Does she have kids?"

"Not that she's said. She came here for a few days to shake off the last vestiges of the relationship with her ex."

"Good Samaritan that you are, you're helping her with that."

"It's a dirty job, but someone has to do it."

"I hate to rain on your parade, rebound guy, but you know Mireya's going to want you to get rid of her as soon as the storm's over."

Ryan was right. Mireya had said as much already. Through the kitchen window I could see the snow still coming down. "But she's here now."

Chapter Seven

I woke to the sound of running water coming from the bathroom. The light was low in the sky. After having the heart-to-heart with Ryan I'd helped him with a few other chores. When I returned to the cabin Allison was still asleep and I was exhausted. The decision to crawl into bed alongside her was an easy one, and I promptly dozed off.

A fire was now roaring in the grate with a fresh log on top. Allison must have added it when she woke up. Since the air still held a slight chill, I surmised she hadn't been awake for long.

The second my feet hit the floor I wished I'd slept with my socks on. If the urge to relieve myself hadn't been compelling, I would have stopped to get dressed. But it was, so I didn't.

The telltale squeal of the pipes told me Allison had just turned off the taps to the bath. Upon opening the door I saw her, laying in repose in the claw-footed tub, eyes closed, steam rising around her, the expression on her face serene.

I quietly stepped inside and pulled the door to, so the warmth didn't rush out.

"Morning," I yawned.

Allison started. She sat up and reached for the curtain, sloshing water onto the floor in her attempt to yank it closed. She was only partially successful.

"Don't tell me you're suddenly getting shy." I lifted up the lid on the toilet seat, aimed and let go a loud, steady stream. I leaned back, keeping one eye on the commode while the other tried to steal a peek at Allison's tits through the water.

"I'm just giving you privacy," she countered, giving the drape a final tug and closing it completely.

I quickly finished my business, flushed, then washed and dried my hands. With one hand I slowly lifted the fabric aside.

"I'm a guy," I told her. "We're used to pissing without privacy. Scoot up."

"You know, Jake, some women enjoy a little mystery."

"Yeah. That's why I stopped wearing underwear when I went off to college. Ma thought it was a ploy to reduce the amount of laundry I had to do. Really? It was to keep the girls guessing about the whole boxers versus briefs thing. You're not scooting."

Allison moved forward and I climbed in behind her, sitting down and spreading my legs so that there was one along either side of her. She leaned back against my chest and released a contented sigh.

"Enjoying your bath?" I asked.

"I haven't been this relaxed in ages. This isn't at all what I expected to happen when I packed up and headed out here."

"You having regrets?"

"About coming here?"

"About us."

"Not a one."

One of my knees was poking up through the surface of the water. Allison started to draw an invisible pattern on top of it. "You?"

"I don't like the thought of being the rebound guy."

"Rebound guy?"

"The guy you fuck to get over Gavin."

"I'm not having sex with you to get over Gavin."

I reached for the bar of soap and began to create a rich lather. "So why are you having sex with me?"

"Do we have to examine this right now?"

"No. Right now you should just lay back and enjoy your bath." I ran one soapy hand over her breast. "I don't know if you realize it, but you're very, very dirty," I murmured into the shell of her ear.

"Am I?"

I let my other hand dip low, in search of her pussy. "Yes."

"Jake." Her breath hitched in excitement as her hips lifted off the bottom of the bath.

The hard tips of her tits broke the surface of the water, warm and rosy. I rolled her left nipple between my thumb and forefinger, pinching it perhaps a bit more firmly than I should have and eliciting a moan that encouraged me to do it again, this time just a little bit harder.

"Does that feel good?" I took her earlobe between my teeth, tugging it playfully.

"Yes," she hissed.

"You like what I do to you." I slipped two of my fingers inside her.

Allison reached back, winding her hand around my neck and threading her fingers through my hair.

I pressed my thumb against her clit, relishing the way she arched her back. She gasped, the sharp intake of breath spurring me on, making my cock nice and hard.

"You want me...again."

"Of course I do. Can't look at you without wanting you. Touching you like this. Christ, I can't seem to get enough of you."

I disengaged from her just long enough to wrap one arm around her waist, then I stood up in the bath, dragging her with me. Water sluiced down our bodies and splashed out onto the bathroom floor. I didn't care.

"What—"

Before she could finish I spun her around to face me, her body flush to mine and my cock trapped between us.

"I have to be inside you," I confessed, lifting her up. Allison wrapped her legs around my waist and, reaching up, she grasped one of the rough sawn timber beams that spanned the length of the ceiling.

"Jake!" She might have said more. I'll never know. The remainder of her words spilled into my mouth, devoured by hungry kisses. My tongue tangled around hers, sliding in and out and around.

Her excitement was building along with mine. I wanted to be inside her. *It* wanted to be inside her. The beast was there, just below the surface. The instant that realization hit me I broke off the kiss.

"Don't stop," she murmured into my ear, before sucking firmly on the flesh. "For God's sake, don't stop."

With a primal growl I pinned her between the wall and me. Then, with one sure thrust I buried myself inside her.

"Fuck!" she gasped, eyes wide, chest heaving, cunt clenching. She came hard and fast, but it wasn't the end.

"I'll fuck you," I promised her, continuing the dance, rocking my hips back and forth, sliding my dick in and out of her. My long, slow strokes had her whimpering.

"I can't hold on." Allison trembled, her body glistening with a thin sheen of sweat that left it almost as slick as her delicious pussy.

"Come with me. I've got you."

She released her hold on the beam. "Don't let me go."

"Never." I crushed my lips to hers once again. Hell, the girl was so amazing, I would have promised her anything. "Come with me, darlin'."

She wound her arms around my neck and grabbed a handful of my hair and pulled, forcing my head back. As soon as we separated she gasped for air, taking it in great big gulps. "I can't. I can't."

"Yes, you can," I assured her. And she did. Then she passed out.

"Easy, cowboy."

Allison was stretched out, in all her naked glory, on my bed. I was trying to convince her to drink more water. She'd downed the first glass without protest. She'd sipped the second one while we talked quietly about nothing and everything. Now she steadfastly refused to accept a third.

"Are you trying to drown me?"

"No. Apparently my sinister plan includes fucking you to death."

"Hmm." She stretched like a cat. "What a way to go."

"Seriously, you scared me. You need water and food and rest and no more fucking."

I hadn't taken the time to get dressed and Allison had noticed, inching her hand up the length of my thigh.

"No more fucking?" She pouted as she wound her hand around the base of my cock.

I closed my eyes and for a moment I imagined her taking me into her mouth, sucking and pulling until I was long and hard for her.

"Not today. But if you're a good little girl tonight and play by the rules, I'll fuck you again in the morning."

She pushed me away with a light shove and rolled over onto her side. "You are a silver-tongued devil."

I slipped on a pair of sweatpants, slid a T-shirt on over my head, then stepped into my tennis shoes. "And, after I fuck you," I told her, as I bent down to lace them up, "I'll lick you with this silver tongue."

"Where will you lick me?"

I walked over and sat on the edge of the bed. "Everywhere. Anywhere. Wherever you want."

"Where are you going?"

"To find you some clothes that will fit. You're about the same size as Mireya."

"Who's Mireya?"

"She lives here on the ranch. I'm sure she wouldn't mind lending you something." I lifted her hand to my mouth and tenderly kissed it. "I'll be back before you know it."

"Then what?"

I looked out the window. The snowfall seemed lighter than it was the last time I'd gone out.

"The storm seems to be dying down. I thought maybe we could head over to the ranch house and help get dinner started. I'm less likely to molest you with other people around."

"In that case, I think it's a horrible idea. We should stay here, and naked."

I picked up my coat, slipped it on, then walked over and opened the cabin door. Before stepping outside I turned back to face her. Allison's hair flowed freely, cascading down her shoulders. The bed covers were rumpled and warm and smelled like us.

"I like you."

She broke off eye contact for a second and nervously licked her lips. "I bet you say that to all the girls."

The fire in the grate snapped and popped. I was aware I was letting the cold air inside, but I couldn't seem to pull myself away.

"No," I confessed finally. "You're special."

Chapter Eight

"You sure it's all right for us to be here?" Allison hovered around the door, seeming hesitant to follow me into the kitchen.

"Positive," I reiterated for the third time. "I'm telling you, the owners of this place are friends of mine. They're kind of like family."

I opened up the enormous refrigerator and peered inside. "Hungry?" Reaching for one of many plastic containers, I popped the lid open and sniffed the contents.

"Starving!" Allison unbuttoned her coat and hung it on the peg by the door. Underneath she had on the pair of Mireya's jeans I'd found in the laundry room and the shirt of mine she'd swiped last night. "What is it?"

"Looks like chili, smells like chili," I reached up for one of the small pots that hung from the rack above the island and placed it on the stove, "I'm thinking it might be chili. Hand me a ladle?" I pointed to the large ceramic pitcher on the island. It held a variety of cooking utensils.

"That would be this thing, right?"

"I take it you don't spend a lot of time in the kitchen." I made fast work of pouring out the mixture and lighting a flame under it.

"Gavin and I used to travel quite a bit. We practically lived in hotels. After the break-up, well, I didn't feel much like eating. I used to enjoy cooking, once upon a time."

"You and Ryan will get along just fine."

"Who's Ryan?" Allison took a seat at the enormous pine table.

"He lives here year-round on the ranch along with the others."

"Others?"

"All in all there's Dakota, Samuel, Mireya, Wright and Ryan. Ryan's the one who does all the cooking. It's off-season now, so he only has a few mouths to feed. You should see this place in the summer. It's hopping."

"Tell me about this place. How did you become friends with the owners?"

I walked over to the sink and started to wash the dirty container, stalling for time and wondering how much I could, or should, divulge.

"I came out here with my father and brother, it was meant to be a family vacation. Only two days into it Dwight Johnson was arrested and my father got called back to the office."

"I remember that case. He played for Dallas right? He was accused of raping and murdering some woman?"

"Yeah. The victim started a relationship online with this guy in a chat room. She thought it was Dwight. It wasn't. They found her body in a hotel downtown. When her roommate was questioned she told the cops Dwight had picked her up the day before. One of the detectives leaked it to the media. It was a circus. Dwight had an alibi, but that didn't seem to matter. For days they all ran with the story."

"You're Walter Madison's son?"

"You know my father?"

She shook her head. "Just by reputation. So, your father went back to Dallas and you and your brother stayed here?"

"Yeah. We should have gone back with Dad, but we didn't. Ross wanted to stay. He'd started up something with a waitress in town. She couldn't resist his charm," I said, a hint of resentment creeping into my voice.

"He can't possibly be more charming than you."

I tossed the dish into the drying rack, wiped my hands off, then made my way over to where she was sitting. I slid my arm behind her back and pulled her out of the chair, tugging her firmly against me.

"'Course not, nobody's as charming as me," I growled playfully, leaning down to nuzzle her neck. "Or as smart, or as good-looking, or as good at fuck—"

Allison pushed me away, laughing. "You're pretty sure of yourself, Dallas."

I used to be and now, with her, I was starting to feel sure of myself again. But then I remembered the path we were going down and the fact that at the end of it, there was going to be a lie.

I strolled over to the fridge. "Want a beer?"

"Why not? I'm on vacation after all."

I cracked two bottles open, tossing the caps into the trash and gave Allison one.

"The short story is one night we went to the bar where the gal worked. We both had more than a few drinks. I left around midnight, Ross stayed."

"To charm the waitress."

"Exactly. When I left the bar he tossed me the keys to the car and promised to meet me in the morning. We had a climb planned for the next day. But Ross didn't show."

"What happened?"

"I went on without him. It was stupid, I know, climbing alone, but that's what I did."

Allison hopped up onto the counter. She was listening intently. "And?"

"I was rappelling down La Pared. I'd made the climb before and I figured I could do it, no problem."

"But there was a problem."

"Yeah." I took a few sips of the beer. It was cold, it tasted good, and it took the edge off.

"Things were going fine," I continued, "then suddenly I came to, bloody and a bit broken. I don't even remember falling. I had a pretty good gash on my head, a dislocated shoulder, and a broken leg. Near as I can figure, a rock fell from above and knocked me out."

"Oh my God! How far did you fall?"

"I don't want to think about it. Night came. I thought I was going to die. I would have, too, if it hadn't been for Ryan." As I finished the sentence I almost choked on the words. This time, it wasn't from bitterness. I drank down the rest of the beer in several long swallows.

"The cook?"

"He was out hiking with Mireya and they stumbled across me."

"They were hiking in the dark?"

I realized my mistake too late and had to think fast.

"When they first spotted me, it was still light outside. Just like I had to do with you, they had to come back to the ranch and return with the right equipment and help."

"You must have been terrified."

"I don't remember a lot. I was slipping in and out of consciousness. Mireya's a nurse; she set my shoulder and splinted my leg. Somehow they got me to a hospital."

"How long were you there?"

"I was there for quite a while. Then I stayed here for a couple weeks before flying home. I guess we all..."

"Became friends?"

"Sort of, yeah. They'll be back soon. You'll get to meet them."

A thick blanket of silence fell over the room.

"We don't have to talk about this if you don't want to," she said softly.

"Thought you shrinks were big on talking." I grabbed another beer from the fridge.

"I'm not your shrink, Dallas. I'm your..."

"My what?" I tossed the beer cap into the trash and tipped the bottle to my mouth. She was peeling the label off hers and had hardly touched it.

"Your friend."

"You're more than a friend. I don't have sex with my friends."

Allison's eyes connected with mine. "*More* than a friend? You going sweet on me, Dallas? I thought we were just fucking."

"Just fucking?" I practically shouted, clutching at my chest. "*Just* fucking? You wound me! My poor, bruised ego. Seriously, woman—"

"Snow's starting to come down hard again. A couple more hours of this and the roads will be closed," Ryan announced, opening the door. Wright was the first one through, followed closely by Mireya. Their arms were full of groceries and within seconds the countertops were covered with an array of bags.

"Miranda?" Allison hopped off the counter.

Something passed between the two of them, an almost imperceptible look of recognition, then panic.

"I mean, Mireya," Allison said, extending her hand. "I'm awful with names. I should introduce myself. Allison Connelly."

"Nice to meet you." Mireya accepted Allison's hand. When she did, I noticed hers was shaking.

"What's wrong?" Ryan asked.

"Nothing," Mireya replied. "Something smells good." She walked over to the stove and gave the pot a stir.

"Ryan's famous chili," I volunteered.

"Don't bullshit me. Something's upset you," Ryan pushed.

"I'm going to go shower," Mireya said, lifting the spoon from the pot and laying it down in the spoon rest.

As she turned to walk away Ryan boldly reached out for her hand. "But we're having dinner together? You promised."

Mireya spared a glance in Allison's direction. "I'm not sure that's a good idea."

"I am," he said, taking a step closer, not backing down. *"I'm sure."*

Her gaze dropped to their still entwined fingers. As soon as it did, Ryan let go.

"All right." She started to leave.

"Six o'clock," Ryan said just as she reached the threshold.

Mireya paused. "Six o'clock," she agreed, not bothering to turn around. Then, before she walked away, she added, "We'll all have dinner together."

"Can I go watch TV?" Wright asked.

"Sure." Ryan never took his eyes off the door.

Wright left the room and I started to pull some bowls from the cupboard.

"Want some chili?" I asked Ryan.

"No."

He suddenly looked forlorn. Obviously, he'd been hoping for a more intimate dinner.

"We don't have to eat here tonight. We can even keep Wright busy if you want. Take him into town for pizza and a movie or something."

"Don't be ridiculous. The weather's going to shit again. The roads are practically impassable." Ryan pulled a big roasting pan out and set it a little too forcefully on the counter. I'd never seen him quite so tense. "What was that about?" he asked Allison.

"Ryan, this is Allison. Allison, Ryan," I interjected.

"I know who she is," he snapped as he fished a sizable package wrapped in brown butcher paper out of one of the sacks and dropped it onto the counter.

"What's wrong? What did I miss?" I asked him while I served up the chili.

Ryan was across from me, on the other side of the island. When I asked the question his head snapped up, concern evident in his face. *"Mireya feels threatened by her. Couldn't you feel it?"*

"I felt something. I don't know her as well as you do. Why on earth would she feel threatened by—"

I think we both became aware of it at the same time, the stench of fear. It was almost overpowering. We both turned to Allison.

"Allison?"

Every muscle was tense and ready, every fiber of her being preparing itself. I could see it, smell it. Hell, I could practically taste it. She looked at me with sheer terror in her eyes. Then I watched in horror as my impressions were realized. She bolted for the door. Pushing through it, she raced out blindly into the storm. No coat. No boots. She was being driven by pure adrenalin, fight or flight. She knew a fight with us was something she had no chance of winning.

"She knows," Ryan said.

I didn't think. I reacted. She was running and I had to follow, catch her. The snow outside was mixed with rain now and the temperature with the wind chill was far below freezing. She'd set off down the driveway toward the road. Slipping on the ice, she went down.

"Allison!" I sprinted after her.

She tried to get up, but in her haste she slipped again, this time listing to the side and falling into a bank of hard pack covered with fresh powder. By that time I'd caught up with her.

"Let me help you."

I reached out for her and she scrambled away. She was panting from exertion, her breath freezing on the evening air. Her eyes were wild, her hair and clothes wet and crusted with snow.

I pounced, covering her with my body, quickly pinning her to the ground. The air was pushed from her lungs in a sudden rush. Bracing myself with my arms, I rose up and stared into her eyes.

"Stop struggling! Don't be afraid!" I snarled, although I understood why she was, and knew my chasing her, dominating her in this way was making it worse. I couldn't seem to help myself, to get control, any more than she could.

She continued to fight me, her body writhing, rubbing up against me.

Mine started to respond to hers. It shouldn't have. She was trembling, afraid. That shouldn't have been arousing, but it was, terribly arousing. In the moment I told myself I was responding to the memory of how, just hours before, our bodies had been locked passionately together. It was more complicated than that though, much more complicated.

Unwittingly, Allison had set something in motion, a hunt so tempting, so enticing, my beast couldn't resist. The chase was short, but it was sweet and the wolf inside me knew what the prize was, intimately. He wanted it. He wanted her. I could feel the wolf as it roiled inside me, demanding escape. I snapped at the wind, devouring the scent of her in greedy gulps.

"Let me go!" she cried out, tears streaming down her face.

A part of me wanted to, knew I should, but there was another part of me that didn't. Even more alarming, it couldn't.

"Jake! Let her go, now!" I wasn't sure who'd said it. And I wasn't about to take the time to find out. I had bigger fish to fry. The sun was setting and the moon was on the rise. I was holding on by a mere thread, one that was quickly unraveling.

I sensed the attack coming, but not in enough time to fend it off. I'd been too distracted, too focused on controlling the struggle with my beast to embrace its innate power. Claws pierced my back and I cried out in pain. They dug deep into my flesh, peeling it away and latching on. A ferocious growl echoed in my ear and I answered it with one of my own.

Rearing up, I released my prey. My attention shifted to defend against the onslaught. I rolled and for a moment the wolf was beneath me. I was strong, but it was stronger. Twisting, its hind legs were flailing against my calves, searching for purchase, trying to get the leverage it needed.

I could feel my bones straining, my skin stretching. I tried to ride the sensation rather than resist it, knowing my only chance at victory would be to do so.

"Jake!" This time is was Allison's voice.

I turned to her, filled with dread about what I would see reflected in her face. Disgust? Revulsion? I never got the chance to see anything.

Suddenly I was catapulted through the air. The world whipped by, a cold, icy blur. I hit something, the side of the house, I think. Then I was down, flat on my back, the wolf on my chest, its vise-like jaws closing in on my neck, clamping down, biting. I could smell my own blood, taste my own failure. The snow swirled overhead. I gazed up at the moon and glimpsed my own death.

"No!" Allison sobbed. "Oh, God! Stop! No!"

"Allison!" I called out to her, but no one heard. The darkness swallowed me.

Chapter Nine

When I regained consciousness I heard voices nearby, speaking in hushed tones. I didn't recognize them at first. I didn't even recognize where I was. My limbs were heavy, my head fuzzy. I was reminded of the time I woke up in the hospital, after the accident. I turned my head to the side and winced. The memories came flooding back and I was overwhelmed with nausea.

"Jake?"

I squeezed my eyes shut. I didn't want to see Allison. I didn't want to face her. My throat was parched. I ached all over. I was certain I'd lost a lot of blood.

The air stirred as she moved closer. "Can I get you something?"

I wanted to tell her to get back, to stay away because I wasn't safe to be around. Only when I lifted my head to speak, my entire universe shifted. I was in a bad way and I knew it. I'd been attacked while I was still in human form and had passed out before I could transform and heal myself.

I swallowed down the bile that had risen, burning the back of my throat and shook my head.

"Maybe a glass of water?" she persisted.

I thought about what Ryan had said earlier about Dakota, about how after the massacre he hadn't been strong enough to change and mend. Was I strong enough to complete the transformation and heal myself? If Allison hadn't been there, I might have given it a try.

I looked away, unable to bear the scrutiny. "I'm so—"

"Hush." She placed her hand gently on the side of my face. "You're a good man, Jake." Her tone was laced with pity. "I'm sorry this happened to you."

"To me? I'm worried about you."

"I'm fine."

She'd been lucky. We'd both been lucky. "I'm surprised you're still here," I managed to croak out while I stared up at the ceiling.

"Quite honestly, so am I."

She sat on the edge of the sofa, the curve of her hip pressing into my side.

"Why are you?" I resisted the urge to reach out and touch her.

"Miranda. I trust her. She explained some things."

"Miranda?"

"Sorry. It's hard to break old habits. Miranda is Mireya's real name."

"What do you mean, her real name?"

"It's kind of a long story. You feeling up to it?"

"Maybe I'll take you up on that glass of water first."

Allison smiled, softly. "Be right back."

As soon as she cleared the room I tried to sit up. It was slow going.

"Take it easy" Allison walked back in carrying a glass of water. When I reached for it, I noticed my hand was shaking. She noticed too.

"Let me help you." She sat down alongside me.

"I can manage. How do you know Mireya?" I took a few sips of the water before handing her back the glass.

"From a case I worked on over a year ago. She was the prosecution's star witness. I was working for the defense. After the defendant escaped, she was placed in a witness protection program."

"That's why she freaked when she saw you?"

"I'd say we both freaked a little. When Miranda walked through the door it caught me by surprise, I slipped. I shouldn't have, but I did. In another situation it might have cost her her life."

"What kind of a criminal case?"

Allison shook her head. "She'll explain. Right now she's a bit shaken. Ryan's with her."

"*She's* shaken?" I laughed ruefully as I fingered the bandage covering my throat."

"It's probably fair to say we're all a bit shaken."

My head was spinning. "You knew Mireya was Were?"

"Yes. At first I thought she'd just been placed here. It didn't occur to me I'd walked right into a den. Not until I saw you and Ryan standing there, across from one another. That's when it hit me."

"How did you know?"

"I'd observed the internal communications between pack members before. Suddenly I just...knew. I could see it."

"What I really am," I added.

"I've only had one other experience dealing with a male Were, Jake. I reacted to you as if you were him and that isn't fair. You're nothing like Roane Devlin."

"The serial killer? He's Were?"

She nodded.

"And Mireya's involved with him somehow?"

"He was my maker." Mireya entered the room, a steaming mug in her hand. "How are you feeling?"

"A little fuzzy," I admitted. I felt clumsy, foolish, weak.

"I gave you something to sedate you, take the edge off."

"You drugged me?"

"You needed to rest for a few hours. You lost a lot of blood." Mireya sat on the edge of the table across from me. "Look, I'm sorry, but you gave me no choice."

"I know."

"You're strong, Jake. You're strong and you lack control. That's a dangerous combination. You weren't responding to me and you were about to shift while you were on top of Allison. One scratch is all it would have taken. One scratch and—"

It came rushing to me and with blinding clarity I understood what had been at stake, what I'd almost done.

"Oh, God," I groaned. It was too much, the combination of shame, self-loathing and sedative. My stomach churned, then heaved. I leapt up from the sofa and ran down the dark hallway to the bathroom, practically falling through the door.

I landed on my knees in front of the commode and retched. Tears stung my eyes. The back of my throat burned. My stomach turned over. I was sickened by the beast in me. I wanted it gone. I wanted to purge myself of it. But I couldn't. It wouldn't come out. Nothing would come out.

"Let me get you a wash cloth."

The moon was now high in the sky and its glow spilled in through the window behind me, illuminating Allison. She looked concerned, vulnerable and oh so beautiful.

"You need to leave." I didn't want to say it. But it was for the best. I couldn't be trusted, not now. Maybe not ever.

"Miranda...Mireya explained. You don't need to go through this alone, Jake. You've been trying to and, well, it's too much. No one could handle this on their own."

"You don't understand."

"Maybe not, but there are people out there who do. I have this friend, Wesley, he's a psychiatrist and he—"

"I don't need a psychiatrist," I shouted. "I need a fucking exorcist! Do you know what could have happened to you? Do you realize what I almost did? You're a smart lady, Allison. Don't be stupid about this. I'm not worth it. You need to get away from me. I'm no good. I'm messed up."

"We're all a little messed up."

I pushed back and leaned against the wall. My shirt, even the front of my jeans, were covered in dried blood, my dried blood. "This isn't a little thing."

"I'm not saying it is. I'm saying you need help."

"I thought I'd be able to go on, pretending everything was normal. But..."

"What you're going through *is* normal."

My core temperature was rising, my skin crawling. "You need to get out."

"No."

With shaky hands I started to pull at my clothes. The surface of my hands started to ripple. "Leave."

My bones were buckling, my nails growing, turning into fierce-looking claws that sliced through the fabric of the soiled garments, tearing them to shreds. I heard the cracking of my own skull, felt the pain in my jaw, eyes, nose.

"Run!" I snarled. "Run!"

"No." She slammed the door shut and locked it. Then she flipped on the light. "This is who you are."

I could only imagine what she saw. My breaths coming hard and fast now, I tried to stand and face the wall. I was focused on the window and the woods outside. I wanted out. I wanted to run, to escape. But my hands wouldn't work the locks.

"You can control this, Jake." Ryan was in my head, his voice calm and comforting. *"You are the wolf."*

"I'm not running." Instead of stepping back, Allison moved closer. "Running was a mistake. I'm standing my ground."

She laid her hand upon my shoulder.

"You don't need an exorcist. There's nothing evil inside you. You are not a demon."

"I'm no longer a man," I cried out, still struggling with the lock on the window. I felt as if I were suffocating. The muscles in my legs strained to support me. The window flew open. A gust of cold, bracing air blew into the room. Snow mixed with rain fell on my face as I gazed up, at the light of the full moon. A primitive howl erupted from deep within my chest. Then another. And another. And they were answered. I pushed off with my hind legs and flew into the air. Headfirst, I dove through the window, landing on all four paws. The snow was coming down hard and heavy, the wind fierce, blowing a thick bank of clouds across the night sky, obliterating the stars, eclipsing the moon. It didn't matter. I could see in the dark. I knew the dark. And I ran toward it.

Chapter Ten

I stood outside, alone, looking in at them. They were gathered around the table, talking, eating. Physically I felt better than I ever had in my life. I was stronger, more powerful. It was almost as if surviving the attack had increased my abilities, my stamina. I'd hunted and fed 'til I was sated. Then I ran, roaming free for hours before heading back. Still, I was full of energy.

I inhaled, deeply. The fresh smell of pine filled my lungs. My body was slick with sweat and still radiating heat. Tendrils of steam rose off my skin, dissipating into the darkness that surrounded me. The transformation back to human form was virtually effortless this time. Something had changed.

"You challenged your Beta in a blood fight and survived," said Ryan.

"I didn't mean to and I barely survived."

"Doesn't matter, man."

"I'm no longer a man. I haven't been for a long time." The snow continued to fall, melting as it drifted down from the sky to settle on my body.

"No. You're more than a man." Ryan's gaze lifted toward the window. *"Come inside where you belong."*

I laughed. *"Is that where I belong?"*

"For now."

"I'm not sure I can face her."

"You can. You must. You owe her that much."

He was right. I owed Allison that much and a hell of a lot more. Just as I was about to step inside, I sensed movement behind me. Turning, I scented the air. Initially there was nothing but the smell of pines, wood from the fire within and the rich aroma of roasted lamb. Then I caught a whiff of something else.

I narrowed my eyes and peered into the night. A deer sprang out of the forest at the edge of the clearing, a five-point buck, majestic and graceful. It raced swiftly across the newly fallen snow, kicking up fresh powder. Midway across the open meadow it came to a halt as if frozen in time, frozen in place. Its big brown eyes met mine and I saw the fear in them as it sized me up. I knew what the creature saw, something wilder; more powerful.

When I looked back, Mireya and Wright had stopped talking and their eyes, too, were on me. We all sensed it, the possibility of the hunt. The hair on the back of my neck rose and a chill ran through me.

The door to the ranch house flew open. Light from the kitchen flooded the porch. Allison stepped outside, arms wrapped around herself.

"Are you all right?"

At the sound of her voice, the deer scampered away. It was time to face the music. I took a fortifying breath, and followed her inside. "My neck's healed."

It was the most I could say. Emotionally, I was still miles away from all right.

Allison's eyes swept down the length of my body and she blushed. "Let me get you a towel so you can...cover yourself." She grabbed a dishtowel from a nearby countertop.

"I don't think that's going to do the trick," Wright observed, pointing to the small rectangular piece of cloth Allison held in her hands.

Every muscle in my body was hard and pumped. I was sporting a very prominent erection. But it wasn't embarrassing. It wasn't even particularly sexual, really. One thing I learned very early on, shifters can't afford to be modest. For me, learning to deal with the fur had been far more challenging than the exposed flesh.

Ryan used his foot to nudge the chair across from him out. "Sit. Are you still hungry?"

Allison pinched the bridge of her nose and closed her eyes. "I'm the only one here who's uncomfortable with Jake being naked. Aren't I?"

"Yup."

"Pretty much."

"Uh huh."

"You weren't uncomfortable last night," I teased, hoping to recapture the easy, intimate way we'd had with one another.

"Jake!" Her gaze darted to Wright, her discomfort heightened by his presence.

"It's all right, Allison," said Wright. "I know about sex. It's how my mom paid for crack and cable."

The color rose in her cheeks. "Sex is more than a commodity to be bought and sold. It's something special, an experience that can be profoundly connecting when shared between two people that truly care about one another."

He appeared to be listening intently. "Is sex with Jake profound?"

I took the seat Ryan had offered and tried not to smile.

To her credit, Allison didn't bat an eye. "Yes."

"I should be charging you." I wanted to place my arm around her waist and pull her in close, but I figured I should put some pants on first. Mireya seemed to read my mind.

"Wright," she interjected, "run on over to Jake's cabin and bring him back some clothes. Then you need to shower and get in bed. It's getting late."

"Don't you want me to clear the table?"

"Not tonight," she replied. "I'll do it."

Wright rolled his napkin into a ball and tossed it onto his empty plate. "Cool!"

He pushed away from the table, slid on a pair of boots, grabbed his coat off the rack and within seconds was out the door.

"He seems like a good kid. Was he born a lycanthrope?" Allison asked.

"No," Mireya replied, "he was turned just last year, along with his mother."

"So, it wasn't an accident?"

"It wasn't an accident, but it was a mistake. Wright's mother had horrendous taste in men."

"Where is she now?"

"She disappeared. My guess is she's in a drug-filled haze somewhere. She could barely keep things together before they were turned. Wright's been through a lot."

"What about the father?"

"He flew the coop before Wright was even born. We're his family now."

"So young," Allison sighed. "So much to adjust to."

"He's really an amazing kid. Ryan, however, was born a lycanthrope," Mireya volunteered as she stood and reached for his plate.

"Stop." Rising to his feet, he casually placed one hand at the small of Mireya's back, then reached for the dish with the other. "Let me clear and do the dishes. You're tired."

"I can handle it," she protested, refusing to let go.

Ryan lightly caressed the side Mireya's face. "You don't have to be strong all the time, you know. I like taking care of you. Let me."

For a moment she appeared to struggle with the decision.

"This can't go where you want it to." She pushed him away with her words, but she leaned into his touch.

Ryan smiled. "I know. I may be weak, but I'm not a complete fool. I know Samuel's stronger, someday he'll be—"

Mireya shook her head. "I have no interest in Samuel."

"I don't understand."

"Ryan, this can't go where you want it to...because I already have a mate."

The dish fell onto the floor, shattering into a dozen pieces.

Ryan looked like he'd been punched in the gut. Mireya moved to pick up the broken pieces, but he stopped her.

"Leave it! Where is he?"

Tears flooded Mireya's eyes. She looked at Allison, then swallowed, hard. "I don't know where he is. No one knows where he is."

"Do you love him?" asked Ryan.

"I've never loved him. How could I?"

"I don't understand."

"Roane Devlin is more than my maker, was more than my Alpha."

"He's your mate?"

"And a monster! The things he did to me, to those other people..."

"Jesus. You're just telling me this now?"

"I couldn't tell you before. I wanted, no I *needed* for that part of my life to be over. Can't you understand?" Mireya turned to Allison. "Why did you have to come here? I was happy! Now I'm going to have to leave and—"

Ryan grabbed hold of her and pulled her into his embrace. "You're not going anywhere. This is your home. We are your pack. You belong with us." He stepped back and searched her eyes. "You belong with me."

The lights dimmed, then flickered. In the space of a moment, we were plunged into darkness. I pushed back from the table just as Wright came through the doorway.

"What happened to the lights?" he asked.

By that time Ryan already had a flashlight in hand. "The power must have been knocked out. We have a back-up generator and plenty of wood. We'll be fine."

He pulled a few candles out of one of the cabinets and set them on the countertop along with a box of matches. Mireya started to light them while I quickly dressed.

"Will the generator kick on automatically?" I asked.

He reached for his coat. "I'm afraid not. If we're lucky I won't have to take a hammer to the damn thing to get it started. I could use you to hold the flashlight."

"You got it." I stepped into my boots, then zipped up my coat and pulled the gloves from the pocket. "Does this happen often?"

"Rarely. But it does happen sometimes."

I followed Ryan outside. The path that had previously been cut from the house to the barn was now covered in a few feet of snow.

"It seems we go through this maybe once a season," he added as we trudged onward. There was a bit of rain mixed in with snow now, and a thin icy crust was forming on top of everything.

We made our way around to the shed behind the barn.

"The generator is in here. Help me clear away some of the snow so we can get the door open." After setting the flashlight down, he started to scoop up and move aside what had piled up in front of the door. I followed suit and in a few minutes we managed to clear the way and pry open the entrance.

The beam of light swept around the room and landed on a small workbench. There was a funnel on top and a large gas can underneath.

"Here." He handed me the flashlight then passed me the funnel. "You hold the funnel in place, I'll pour in the gas."

"Where does it go?"

Ryan pointed my hand in the right direction, so that the beam shined on the opening before he started to unscrew the cap. "Right there."

"Got it."

He lifted the gas can and started to empty the contents into the generator's tank. The sharp smell of fuel hit my nostrils.

"What's it mean, really, that Mireya's mated?" I asked.

"It means she and Devlin are connected to one another, in every way, body and beast," he said. "There's only one way for a mated relationship to end and that's in death."

Ryan set the gas can down on the ground, replaced the cap, then wiped his hands off on a rag.

"You seemed more than surprised by this little revelation. You seemed almost incredulous. I don't know. Almost like you didn't believe her at first. Or maybe it was that you didn't want to believe her."

"Honestly, I don't know how she's managed to hide from him, to mask the connection. It doesn't make sense. Devlin's a ruthless hunter. If he's Were *and* Mireya's mate, I would have expected him to track her by now. I'm afraid I'm at a loss to explain this one."

"Does it change how you feel?"

"Not one lick."

I gave his shoulder a squeeze. "If it's any consolation. She's in love with you."

"You really think so?"

"Yeah. Once more, I'm an idiot for not seeing it sooner."

Ryan pulled out his cell phone. "Still no signal. I hope Samuel and Dakota made it safely to Dalton's Pass."

"You wish they were here."

He looked up at me. "We can't protect them, just the two of us, Jake. Devlin's an Alpha and he's rogue."

"He hasn't tracked her here yet. What makes you think he's going to show up now?"

"I don't know. Humor me. What are we going to do if he does? What are we going to do if he tries to take Mireya, or hurt Allison or Wright? You know what he's capable of."

I didn't even have to think about it. "We kill him."

Ryan switched on the generator, then reached up and gave the pull chain overhead a yank. The bare light bulb attached to it snapped on and the shed was flooded with light.

"You ever kill anyone, Jake?"

"Nope. You?"

Ryan shook his head. "You say it so easily. Do you really think you could kill him?"

"If it was him or me, or to save an innocent life? Yeah. Hell yeah."

"I've never even shot a gun."

"But you hunt."

"As a wolf it's different. I'm just another of God's creatures doing what comes natural. Gun's aren't natural."

"You believe in God?" My question surprised him.

"I do."

"And you really believe he had a hand in creating us, in creating what you are and what I've become?"

"You don't?"

"I used to. Now?" I shook my head. "I don't know. We should inventory weapons, just in case."

"All those rifles in the cabinet belong to Dakota and Samuel." Ryan opened the door to the shed and peered outside. "The lights in the house are back on. We should be good for the night."

"You know where Dakota keeps the ammo?"

"There's a floor safe in his room. A bullet isn't going to kill Devlin, Jake."

"Not even a silver one?"

"This isn't the movies." He smiled. "The silver would make it burn like a son-of-a-bitch and slow down the healing process. But one bullet won't kill him."

"How many would it take?"

"I honestly don't know."

I looked over at the can of fuel. "What about a grenade?"

Ryan snapped his fingers. "Damn it, I knew I wanted to save that last grenade for something!"

"How much gas is there here on the ranch?"

"Why?"

"Just thinking out loud."

"I'd say we have plenty to see us through the storm. There's a fuel tank on the east side. We get it filled before winter. It's gotta be getting low by now, but it'll be enough to keep the generator running until we have service again. There's always the option of siphoning more out of my truck, if need be."

"I wasn't thinking about the generator. How about we make crude grenades out of bottles, fill them with fuel, add a bit of silver..."

"Will you stop with the silver? We're werewolves. We use stainless steel. We don't have any goddamned silver."

I raised my hands in surrender. "Sorry."

"We best get back," Ryan said, anxiously looking around. "It's getting late."

The wind whipped about us as we retraced our steps through the snow and back to the house. I had the germ of an idea rolling around in my head. I'd never been one to go looking for a fight and I didn't want one now. But I had a feeling one might be coming. If it was, I wanted to be ready. There was simply too much at risk not to be.

"Hey, you've got a tractor up here, don't you?"

"You kidding? You've seen my garden. You don't think I till it by hand, do you?"

"So there'd be fuel in it, too."

"Uh-huh."

"Didn't you tell me once you make your own fertilizer?"

"Yup. You should have seen my tomatoes last year. I still have some—"

"Do you use nitrogen?"

"On my tomatoes? Some, I mix it in with the maize compost. Not too much though, I like to use—"

"How much do you have?"

"Oh, it was a good crop. I bet you I put up about sixty pounds. How about I make spaghetti tomorrow night? You've never had my Bolognese. *È magnifico.*"

"Sounds great." Ryan was much more at ease now. He'd rather talk about cooking than killing any day of the week. I almost hated to ask my next question. Unfortunately, we were almost to the porch. It was now or never. If I didn't get to the point, soon he'd be launching into the recipe and we'd be having this conversation within earshot of the girls. "How much of the fertilizer do you have?"

"We've been using more and more organic. I'm really starting to worry about my carbon footprint, you know? I'll probably never have kids, but still—"

I got impatient. "Ryan!"

He stopped dead in his tracks. We were just a few feet from the steps.

"How much of the fertilizer do you have? More than a couple pounds?"

"Yeah. Why? I've probably got close to forty."

"Where?"

"In the garden shed north of your cabin."

I looked around. The snow was falling harder. Visibility was poor.

"When I was out earlier, I was able to see fine. Now I can barely see the edge of the clearing."

"You should stay in the main house with us tonight," Ryan suggested. He unlocked the front door then kicked the side of the threshold, knocking snow off his boots.

I paused. "So you can keep an eye on me?"

"I was thinking we'd be keeping an eye on one another."

"Bullshit. You don't trust me around Allison." I meant for it to sound indignant, but couldn't quite muster up the self-confidence to pull that one off. The truth was, I didn't know if I could trust myself around Allison.

"There's safety in numbers, Jake. Plus, we need to conserve fuel right now. I think we should sleep in shifts, just in case. Devlin's more likely to attack at night, when he's at peak strength."

"And tomorrow night, during the full moon, he'll be at his strongest."

Ryan nodded.

I glanced back over my shoulder. "We need to be ready for him. Do you suppose Dakota and Samuel will be back by tomorrow night?"

"Doubtful."

"You think you can count on me to maintain control if there's a fight?"

Ryan grinned. "Buddy, I'm counting on just the opposite."

"I don't understand."

He reached around, grabbed the back of my neck, and pulled my head down until my forehead touched his.

"What do I smell like, Jake?"

I started to pull away, but he was surprisingly strong and held me in place.

"Close your eyes. Breathe me in. You know this scent."

I shut my eyes and inhaled. I could smell traces of wine on his breath. Rosemary. Garlic. The mint mouthwash he'd used after dinner. There was a lingering odor from the gasoline he'd spilled on his hands. Underneath that a citrus soap. Orange. Then there was something else I recognized.

"Pack," I whispered into the quiet space between us. "You smell like pack."

Ryan pulled back and smiled. "You're bonded to me, to this pack, by an invisible thread. It will always be there. Follow it and you'll find me, find us."

"How?"

"When you need it, you'll figure it out. No one had to explain to you how to breathe, did they?"

"Is that how you think Devlin is going to track Mireya? Come on, Ryan. Sure, I can recognize your scent and tell you're pack. You're standing right in front of me."

"It's not just about scent. It's about something intangible, mystical."

"No way could I track you down in another town, another—"

"Maybe not now. Maybe not ever. Trust me though, for some it's possible. The bond between maker and Were is stronger than the one between pack members in general. The bond between mates is even stronger. Devlin is Mireya's maker and her mate."

A thought occurred to me.

"It works both ways, doesn't it? Mireya would be able to sense him too, right?"

"Theoretically, but she must be doing her damndest to cut herself off from him. It's almost as if she's been metaphysically cleansed or something. Normally you can sense when a woman is mated and I had no idea."

"Think. Not even a hint?"

"Lately I noticed..." He shook his head. "I thought she and Samuel had become involved. Now I wonder if it was something else. Or possibly *someone* else."

"Devlin? You think maybe he's been trying to connect with her somehow?"

"You'd think if he was, she'd know it. I can't put my finger on it, but something doesn't seem right about this whole thing. It just doesn't add up."

He opened the kitchen door and a gust of warm air rushed out. "You and Allison gonna share? I can put Wright in Samuel's room. Then the two of you can sleep in his room."

I meant to follow Ryan inside, but the question he had posed stopped me. The events from earlier in the day were still too fresh, the confidence in my ability to control myself too shaky. I needed a bit more time and distance.

"You go on inside. Find out exactly how much ammo we have."

Ryan raised an eyebrow. "Where are you going?"

"The garden shed. I want to check something out. I won't be long. Look, it'll be less awkward if you can work out the sleeping arrangements without my being there. Allison's a wonderful lady."

"She seems to be. So why are you pulling away from her?"

"I couldn't see my way clear to tell her the truth. She didn't deserve to be lied to."

"You didn't lie to her."

"I wasn't honest."

"You couldn't be. She knows the score. She realizes that."

"I can't stomach the idea of hurting her. Go on and put Allison in Samuel's room. No sense in disturbing Wright. I'll be fine on the sofa. Be back in a bit."

I turned to leave but, before I could walk away, Ryan reached out and grabbed me. "Putting Allison in Samuel's bed is not a good idea."

"She's already settled in my room." Mireya padded barefoot across the floor. She wore a pair of black silk pajamas, her hair hanging loose about her shoulders. "I'm pretty sure she's expecting you to join her. Come in from the cold, Jake." Not even sparing me a glance, she walked up to Ryan and her gaze locked with his. Something passed between them, but whatever it was, it wasn't meant for me and I wasn't privy to it.

"Are you sure?" Ryan reached up hesitantly.

Mireya nodded. "I'm sure."

I was glad someone was. I wasn't. I wasn't sure of much of anything. Except for maybe what I was going to do with the fertilizer. My mother had grown up in Oklahoma City and had been visiting during the spring of 1995. She'd been just a few blocks away at the Piggly Wiggly when the Murrah Federal Building exploded. Growing up, I'd heard stories, seen pictures. I knew what ANFO could do and I knew if the going got tough, we could count on it for some protection. *That* I was sure of.

Chapter Eleven

Hours had passed and despite the cold I was now drenched in sweat from exertion. I packed the final bit of snow around the last of the five-gallon water jugs, then paused to admire my handiwork. I'd circled the house, spacing the jugs along the outside perimeter about fifteen feet apart, each one within view of a window. One carefully placed shot and...

"Can I ask what you're doing?"

My heart caught in my throat. I spun, rising quickly to my full height, every muscle in my body tensed and ready.

I'd seen pictures of Devlin and this wasn't him. There was a flicker of recognition. "Mac?"

He shook his head. "Dell. People make that mistake all the time. Dell Renfield."

I'd met him briefly, a couple months prior. His father, Byron, had me flown to Canada. Then he made me an offer he thought I wouldn't refuse. Only I did.

"It's the middle of the night," he said. "Shouldn't you be tucked in bed?"

Like his father, Dell was a vampire. How old of one, I didn't know. What I did know was that he was different from the last time we'd met. But then, so was I.

"You're wasting your time coming here. Tell your father my answer's the same now as it was before."

Byron took a big risk when he invited me into his home, into his world. He took an even bigger risk letting me walk out of it. Yet he did. No strings attached, nothing but an open invitation to return. It had seemed too good to be true at the time, now it seemed the proverbial noose was tightening. The timing couldn't have been worse. The last thing I needed was to get into a pissing contest with a goddamned vampire.

"I'm not here to do my father's bidding."

Dell's black leather duster was unbuttoned and the wind lifted it so that it billowed out and whipped behind him like a cape. He wore no hat, no gloves. His jet-black hair was covered with snow but he didn't seem to notice or mind.

"Why are you here?"

"I'm with the PSF, Jake. I came on business of my own."

"What kind of business and what's the PSF?"

"Wow. You are still new to all of this, aren't you?"

He didn't look like he'd hiked in. He wasn't dressed for it. The road closures should have made driving in impossible at this point and I hadn't heard any approaching vehicles.

"I'll trade you stories for a drink. I could use a little something to warm me up." A layer of snow had accumulated atop his head and he casually brushed it off.

"I can make us a pot of fresh coffee."

"I was thinking more along the lines of a single malt."

"You're on." Reaching into my pocket, I pulled out the last of what was left—two bits of coal and a half of a carrot. I placed them on the ball of snow I'd made earlier and positioned it on top of the mound.

"Vampires aren't really bothered by the cold you know."

"No?"

He shrugged. "I mostly wanted the drink."

"You didn't come here for a drink."

Dell shoved his hands into his pockets and turned to survey the army of snowmen surrounding the house. "You know what I do when I can't sleep?"

"What?"

"Read." He gave me a sideways glance. "The full moon got you twitchy?"

I started to walk back to the house and he followed. "It's not full until tomorrow, but yeah. Though I feel better now. Usually I go for a long run when I'm like this. In this weather? I thought it'd be best to stay close to home."

"The sun will be up soon."

I paused in front of the door. "Is that a problem for you?"

Dell shook his head. "No. I take Protectus."

"It exists? I thought that was a myth."

"It's expensive, and hard to get, but it's out there."

"Would it help me?"

Dell placed his hand on my shoulder and gave it a little squeeze. "Sorry, no. The medical research division of the Academy is working on something, though. It's tricky business. Seems it's easier to test out new things on immortals—no harm, no foul. It's harder with shifters. It's still all pretty theoretical right now and *way* over my head."

I was still trying to wrap my head around it, the differences between reality and the long-standing myths. Vampires weren't undead. They were born and immortal, impervious, able to live forever. Unless they broke a very important and sacred rule— mating with a human. Then they were fucked.

I opened the door. "Do I need to invite you in?" The look of amusement on his face gave me my answer. "Really, they should give out a handbook or something."

"You didn't get the handbook? What kind of a two-bit pack did you join?" He followed me through the door and into the kitchen,

I removed my hat, gloves and coat, tossing them on the counter. Then I walked over to the cupboard on the far side of the kitchen and pulled out a bottle of scotch.

I gestured toward the cabinet next to the sink. "Glasses are in there."

Dell grabbed two and we met at the table. My face burned from the cold, my hair was dripping wet, and the legs of my jeans were crusted over with snow and sticking uncomfortably to my legs. Dell looked like he'd walked out of a trendy men's fashion magazine.

I poured him a generous amount of scotch and mulled over what he'd just told me.

"I'd like to learn more about the research you mentioned," I said.

"My father would be able to explain it far better than I could."

"I'm not sure I'm willing to risk another conversation with your father. He's a hard man to say no to."

"He is annoyingly persistent."

"All I want to do is finish school and live a normal life."

"And are you?"

The directness of his question caught me off guard. "Am I what?"

"Living a normal life?"

I stared at the amber liquid in my glass for a moment before responding. "No. But I'm trying and I'm gonna keep trying."

"To persistence," Dell raised his glass.

"To persistence."

"What is normal anyway?"

I swallowed the scotch I still held in my mouth before responding. "You think I'm a fool for saying no."

"Fools aren't invited to attend the Academy."

"Why was I invited?"

"Dad didn't tell you?"

I shook my head.

"You met a...certain profile. For years he's been watching, waiting. An intuitive came to him long ago and—"

"Intuitive?"

"A seer of sorts. You're supposed to be *important.*"

"Me? To what?" I took a sip of the scotch. The rich, smoky liquid scalded on the way down.

"Damned if I know. Possibly the fate of the world."

"Fate of the world?" I scoffed.

"That's usually how these things work."

"Bullshit. Look at me."

Dell shrugged. "Maybe. Maybe not."

"I don't mind telling you, Dell, I'm pretty fucked up right now. I'm no use to anyone. I'm barely keeping my head above water as it is. Half the time I feel like I'm walking around in some crazy dream and I can't wake up."

"As my mother would say, 'we all have issues'."

"Issues?" I could hardly suppress my laughter. It might have been the scotch combined with a lack of sleep. The entire situation seemed ludicrous. "Okay, make me feel better. Tell me, what's your big issue?"

Dell set his glass down on the table and leaned forward. "I think I've met the love of my life. She's human. I'm afraid to commit. If I don't, I think I might lose her. If I do, then..."

"Bye-bye eternity."

"Right."

Human mates were the Achilles heel of the immortals, the one thing that made them vulnerable. That I knew. Just like with Weres, once mated, their mortal coils were irrevocably linked. The difference was, vampires couldn't escape that bond in death. Upon the end of his mate's life, a vampire would be dragged into death by it.

"How old are you?"

"Soon I'll be twenty-six."

"Fuck."

"Feel better?"

"Yes. But I'm still not ready to sign on with the Academy."

"I already told you, that's not why I'm here." Dell took a sip of his drink, then picked up the bottle and looked at the label. "Good stuff."

"It belongs to Samuel, my Beta. Have as much as you want."

Dell smiled. "I'm liking you more and more."

A moment passed, then another. "What did bring you here?" I finally asked.

Dell stood and removed his coat. His hair had grown a bit since the last time I'd seen him. It was almost shoulder length now.

"I've actually been here for a few hours. I arrived just as you and the other one were leaving the house. I've been following you, trying to decide."

"Decide what?"

He stared down into the glass. "How much to tell you."

"About?"

He looked up at me, his gaze intense, penetrating. "The woman you know as Mireya and Roane Devlin."

"You came here because of them?" He had my full attention.

"Do you know what a mage is, Jake?"

"I have a feeling we aren't talking about a role playing game."

"Before I went to the Academy I trained with one of the most powerful. I was young and he was like a second father to me." He paused, a shadow crossing his face.

"And then?"

"I grew up and saw things more clearly." He took another sip of scotch before continuing. "After the Academy I went to work for the PSF. I found out Basta had been doing some contract work for them."

"You mentioned them earlier. What's the PSF?"

"The Preternatural Special Forces. They are a small contingent of agents like me, agents with *special abilities*. I'm not the only vamp, there are a few others. We've got shapeshifters, several fairies, a few ghosts, a couple succubi, and we just recruited our first angel."

"You can do magic?" I asked.

"Yes."

"What kind of magic?"

"Powerful magic."

"More powerful than Thrall?"

Dell scoffed. "Please! That's child's play. Any vampire truly worth his salt can do Thrall."

"And this Basta guy and you both work for the PSF?"

"Basta used to work for the PSF. Not anymore."

"He quit?"

"I killed him."

A cold chill ran down my spine. He said it so matter-of-factly. I wanted to know more. I wanted to know why. But the question stuck in my throat. Dell must have sensed my discomfort.

"I had no choice. I did what I had to do," he volunteered before downing the rest of the scotch and setting the glass down on the table. "I did what any man would do, under the circumstances. My only regret is there were some unexpected consequences."

"Consequences?" I wondered if they had anything to do with the change I sensed in him, the shift in power.

He sighed and his shoulders sagged. Then, under his breath he added, "When dark magic is involved there are always consequences."

"What kind of consequences are we talking about?"

Dell leaned back in his chair. "When Basta died, much of his magic died with him."

"I'm not sure I understand. What does this have to do with Mireya?"

"Unscrupulous bastard that he was, unless the person specified differently, upon Basta's death all of his spells went poof."

"Poof?"

"When your Mireya was placed into the witness protection program, Basta was the one who created her protective shield. It's what's been cloaking her, keeping her hidden from the big, bad wolf. The shield has been down for a while, Jake. Two months, maybe more."

"It's back up now?"

"Yes. That's why I came, to put it back in place."

"This shield, you're sure it will keep her safe?"

"It was designed to block the metaphysical connection between her and Devlin. Hopefully that will be enough. There are no other special protections, nothing to guarantee her safety should he find her."

I was out of my element. My eyes felt tired and gritty from lack of sleep. I wasn't thinking as clearly as I normally did. I wasn't sure what was even possible.

"Could there be?" I asked him. "Could you do something to guarantee her safety? Is there such a thing?"

"There are stronger magics, certainly, but a guarantee? You're talking about messing with fate on an entirely different level. You don't understand what you're asking," Dell replied.

"How long were the shields down?"

It was Allison. She was wearing an oversized T-shirt I didn't recognize. It ended mid-thigh, leaving her long, shapely legs bare.

"Damn it, Dell. How long were they down?" she pressed.

"You two know each other?" I asked.

"What are you doing here?" Dell's eyes ran down the length of her body.

I felt a flare of jealousy and had to suppress the impulse to tell Allison to go put some clothes on.

"What am *I* doing here? What are *you* doing here?"

Dell leaned back in his chair. "You first. I'm betting your story is far more interesting than mine. That's a new look for you."

Allison reached up and ran her fingers through her tousled hair. "I'm on vacation, actually."

"Vacation?"

"Yes. I was hiking a few miles away. There was an accident out on the trail. Jake found me."

"I see." He subtly scented the air, then turned to face me with a knowing smile.

Allison continued. "This freak storm blew in. By coincidence he happened to be staying here. End of story."

"I don't believe in coincidence," Dell said.

"What's that supposed to mean?" I asked.

"I'm not sure what it all means. And, unfortunately, I don't have the time to sit here and figure it out. I'm needed elsewhere."

"Are you telling me the PSF sent you here just so you could drop this little bomb on us and then fly away?" Allison made a little fluttery motion with her hand.

"Vampires can fly?" They both looked at me as if I were the town idiot.

"No," Dell answered slowly. He turned to Allison and added, "You know I don't *fly*."

"Teleport. Whatever."

Dell frowned. "There's a big difference, you know. Anyway, the answer to your question is close to eight weeks. The shields have been down close to eight weeks."

"Eight weeks?"

"And the PSF didn't send me. They don't know I'm here and, frankly, I'm pretty sure they wouldn't approve."

"I need coffee," Allison said.

"I think Ryan keeps coffee beans in the canister over there." I pointed to the stainless-steel container next to the kitchen sink. "So, teleporting, is that a vampire thing or just a magic thing?"

Allison walked over, grabbed the coffee pot and began filling it with water. "I thought the PSF were the good guys. Why wouldn't they want to uphold their end of the bargain and keep the shields in place?" she asked.

"We are the good guys." Dell looked uncomfortable. "The shields weren't dropped on purpose. I was explaining to Jake before you came in, the mage who erected them is gone, and with him, his magic."

"What do you mean by gone?" Allison asked.

"Dead," I clarified.

"I'm repairing what I can," Dell continued. "I've been given a list of priorities. This job was just added to it. They would have sent me here...eventually."

"Just not today," I added.

"Right."

Allison started the coffee and then began to search the cupboards for cups. "So why are you here instead of following orders like a good little soldier?"

"I guess I'm more of a big picture kind of guy." Dell helped himself to another glass of Samuel's scotch. "Plus, I think I might be trying to get myself fired. You know me, I don't like to quit anything. But I'm not sure the PSF is where I'm supposed to be."

"You'd rather have them fire you than quit?" Allison asked.

Dell appeared to mull over the question. "I think so."

"He has issues," I interjected helpfully.

"I'm not buying this rebel-without-a-cause bullshit," snapped Allison. "You like to give everyone the impression you're flying by the seat of your pants, but I've seen how your mind works. If you wanted to just walk away, you would. You haven't. Yet you're taking risks and not following orders. Why?"

Dell took another sip of his drink. "I've never been all that good about following orders."

Allison was undeterred. "It looks to me like you're working both sides of the fence. Something's up."

"You're right. This is about to get personal for me," Dell said. "Very personal."

"What's happened?" she asked.

"My parents are at risk."

I leaned forward. "Your parents?"

"They need my protection. It was just a matter of time, really. My parents have been surprisingly cooperative up until now. We've known they were prime targets. The island's safe. Between Stanley Houghton, our head of security, and myself, we've seen to that."

"But?" I asked.

"My father's been called to Washington."

Allison's eyes widened. "D.C.?"

"By the President."

That little revelation seemed to surprise her even more. "Why?"

"I don't know. Whatever the reason is? He's keeping it to himself. What I do know is he won't go without my mother and I'm not letting them go without me. As much as I'd like to stay here..."

"I understand," Allison said as she poured a cup of coffee. "Can I get either of you a cup?"

"Count me in." I stood and walked over to her.

She handed me the coffee she'd already poured and in a low voice whispered, "You never came to bed last night."

I blew a stream of cool air across the surface of the cup and took a sip. "I had some things to take care of."

"I thought maybe you were..." Allison glanced over to Dell, then she lowered her voice another notch and added, "avoiding me."

Forbidden: The Temptation

"I can hear you, you know," Dell said as he stood and started to put on his coat. He pointed to his ear. "Vampire. Can't help it. Anyway, I think this is my cue to leave."

"You can't leave without Miranda," Allison insisted. She set her coffee down on the counter. "If the shields were down for as long as you say they were, she's not safe here, Dell. You know it and I know it. She needs to be relocated."

"That's already in process. A new identity's been set up. I imagine someone will be here to collect her and affect the transition tomorrow, or the day after at the latest."

"What if they're too late?" Allison asked. "They should have moved on this already."

"They think Devlin's in Canada."

"There's no sense in the two of you arguing about this. She's not going to leave," I interjected. "And she shouldn't have to. This is her home."

"And she can come back. When it's safe." Allison reached out for Dell. "You have to take her with you."

"I can't. I wish I could, but I can't. If I was at peak power, I'd do it in a heartbeat. But I'm not. And, like it or not, I need to conserve what power I have as best I can. I have to pick and choose my battles, Allison."

"What if your intelligence is wrong? What if he's not in Canada?"

Dell looked down at his shoes and released a heavy sigh.

"You don't believe he's there. You think they've got it all wrong. That's why you're here," Allison said.

Dell nodded. "The kill in Canada doesn't exactly fit the profile. The victim wasn't higher up in the food chain. Some people think he got impatient with the wait. That he had trouble setting up his next kill and out of desperation settled for less."

"What do you think?" I asked.

"I don't think men like Devlin settle. Do you?" He directed the question at Allison.

"No. No, I don't," she replied.

A blanket of silence fell over the room, thick and heavy.

"He's is a crazy bastard, but he's Were, pure and simple," Dell added.

Allison wrapped her arms around herself and shivered. "There's nothing *pure* or *simple* about Devlin. He has one of the most complex and disturbing delusional systems I've ever seen."

"Dell, you said your parents were known targets, you mentioned a profile. I read in the paper Devlin only went after women. I thought there wasn't any rhyme or reason to his choices." I added some sugar to my coffee and gave it a stir. "Isn't the absence of an identifiable killing pattern the very thing that stumped the FBI?"

Dell glanced at the kitchen clock, then turned to Allison. "As much as I'd like to stick around, my father's flight leaves in thirty minutes. I have some things to take care of beforehand."

"Go. I'll explain."

"Thanks." Dell extended his hand and I grasped it. "And thanks for the drink. I'll be in touch. I'm sorry I can't stay."

"Will you contact us if you hear anything more on Devlin?" Allison asked.

"Of course." He walked to the door. "It was good to see you both. Sorry it couldn't have been under better circumstances. Don't rule out the Academy, Jake. Think about what I said."

"They're trying to recruit you for the Academy?" Allison sounded surprised.

A blast of ice-cold air rushed past me. I turned toward it, expecting to see an open doorway, but the door remained closed. And Dell was gone.

Chapter Twelve

"Are you all right?" Allison looked a bit concerned.

Everything felt so surreal. Was it the lack of food and sleep, the scotch, or the fact that I seemed to have slipped down the fucking rabbit hole?

"He can actually teleport to another place, another time?" I asked.

"I don't know about another time. But from one place to another, yes. From what I understand it's a pretty advanced skill for a sorcerer. Some species can do it inherently—ghosts, angels, succubi."

"Unbelievable," I muttered, shaking my head.

Allison pulled a frying pan out of the cupboard and set it on top of the range. "Believe it. Accept it. The sooner you do, the sooner you'll adapt to all of this, Jake."

"I'm trying."

"Try harder."

The edge in her voice made me wince. It wasn't like the Allison I'd gotten to know.

She sighed heavily. "I'm sorry, I don't mean to sound snippy."

"It's all right. We've all been under a lot of stress the past few days."

"I didn't sleep well last night." She walked over to the kitchen window and gazed outside. "I was worried about you. We need to talk."

In my limited experience, nothing good has ever followed those four little words.

I wanted to walk up behind her, to snake my arm around her waist and pull her close. "In case you haven't noticed, I'm better at expressing myself physically."

Allison reached for my hand.

I held my breath. It was the first time she'd touched me since seeing me change.

"We need to agree on a plan and I'm afraid we don't have much time. I'm going to make you breakfast. Then you need to rest."

"No offense, but that doesn't sound like much of a plan."

"The sun is up. If Devlin is around, if he is planning something, it'll happen at night. He'll bide his time until he's at his strongest."

"And I should be rested up."

"Actually, I think by mid-day you, Ryan, Mireya and Wright need to be gone."

I stepped back, breaking our connection. "What? No way."

"The roads might not be drivable, but the four of you don't have to drive. You can shift. I'll stay here and wait for the agent from the Witless Protection Program to show up. When he does I'll tell him he's a couple days late and offer to have Mireya check in with him as soon as she's safe."

Allison faced me, her gaze steady and unwavering. She seemed solid, certain, about as far from a damsel in distress as I could possibly imagine.

"The breakfast I'll accept," I told her. "Once Ryan and Mireya are up, I'll agree to a nap. As for the rest? No way am I leaving you here. You might as well get the notion out of your head right now."

"I don't fit the profile. He won't be interested in me," she argued.

"You can't know that for sure."

"I worked the case, Jake. Dell and I know one another because I'm the one who called in the PSF."

"Am I the only one who doesn't know about the PSF?"

Allison shook her head. "I didn't know about them until the Devlin case. Honestly, when all of this started to unfold, for a while I thought maybe I was losing my mind."

"I know what you mean."

"If it hadn't been for Wesley—"

"The psychiatrist you mentioned yesterday?"

"Yeah."

"How does he figure into all of this?"

"Only peripherally, really. As soon as Devlin was caught he hired James Butler to handle his case."

"I remember seeing that on the news."

"James called in Gavin. I was sent in to profile Devlin." She took a sip of her coffee before continuing. "Right from the start I sensed there was something different about him. I wasn't naïve, I knew all about transference, about boundaries, about professional distance. He was obviously psychotic but..."

"But what?"

"There were parts of Devlin's story I found myself starting to believe. I didn't want to go to Gavin with what I thought he'd just dismiss as crazy suspicions. We'd recently gone through that when I confronted him about the affair. I'd just moved out of the house and I'd given him my notice. Things between the two of us were unbelievably strained."

"So you went to Wesley."

"I agonized over it for days. I'd chosen my words carefully. I didn't need to. Within minutes Wes started finishing my sentences for me. We went and interviewed Devlin together. When I went home that night, my head was spinning."

"I can imagine."

"There was an envelope waiting for me on the front porch, under the doormat. It contained a CD filled with relevant references; digital files of old manuscripts, translations of ancient texts, dozens and dozens of files. And there was a phone number, scribbled on a slip of paper."

"It was the number for the PSF?"

"It was Dell's cell phone. Ten minutes into the call he was suddenly standing in my kitchen. In less than twelve hours my entire world had changed."

"And you accepted it all, just like that?"

"I accepted there's a lot I don't know, a lot I don't understand. But there's one thing I do know. I know Devlin. He wants two things."

"What are they?"

"He wants to live forever and he wants Mireya at his side. If he comes here, it's going to be for Mireya. If you and Ryan are here, he'll see the two of you as a threat. It won't be pretty, Jake. I've seen the photos from the crime scenes."

Allison pulled out a carton of eggs and cracked four of them into a bowl.

"If I'm here and everyone else is gone, he's likely to just turn around and try to pick the trail up as quickly as possible. He'll be suspicious about the coincidence, but I'll stick mostly to the truth and play the empathetic shrink."

I placed my hand over hers. "You'd really send us off and stay here to face Devlin alone?"

"Don't look at me like that. I'm not being brave. I'm being practical," she added as she whipped the eggs vigorously.

"There's just one problem with your plan, darlin'." I pushed the eggs aside, and pulled her to me. "I'm not gonna go along with it."

"Me neither." Ryan picked up the bowl. "I want something a little more special than scrambled eggs. You sit down. I'll make breakfast. I promised Mireya French toast this morning."

"We weren't talking about breakfast, Ryan. We were talking about Devlin," I clarified, releasing Allison.

Ryan waved me off. "We don't have to worry about Devlin. Mireya explained it all to me last night. Some guys in this special forces unit did a bit of mumbo jumbo. He can't find her. She's perfectly safe. Remember last night when I told you it was almost as if she were cleansed or something? Well, that's not far from the truth. Everything's fine. Shit, everything is more than fine, it's goddamned fantastic! You were right, Jake."

"Somebody got laid last night," I teased, reaching out to ruffle the hair on top of his head.

"Cut it out!" Ryan blushed crimson. "You say it so casually. It wasn't like that. It wasn't something common. It was...amazing."

I couldn't remember ever seeing Ryan this happy. The last thing I wanted was to throw a bucket of ice-cold water on his afterglow. The sentiment must have shown on my face.

"What?" Suddenly he looked like he'd been kicked in the stomach. Or maybe I was projecting some.

"It was a shield they placed around her, but something happened to it a couple months ago. The spell was shattered, Ryan. Devlin's had almost an eight-week head start. They want to relocate Mireya as soon as possible. Someone will be coming for her, tomorrow or the next day. Hopefully before Devlin."

Ryan turned to look at Allison, then back at me.

"How do you know this?"

Allison explained, "Someone from the PSF was here and left just a few minutes ago. They reinstated the shield but it could be too late."

"They have reason to believe he's headed this way? Why the hell didn't they remove her?" Ryan walked up to me, fuming. "Why didn't you wake us?"

"There really wasn't time. At first I thought he was here because of me. I'd met him briefly before. A few months ago I had some business with his father. Allison knows him too. He's a..."

"Sorcerer," Allison interjected.

"He was here one minute, gone the next," I added.

Allison poured herself some more coffee. "The authorities think Devlin's in Canada somewhere, but—"

"But what?" Ryan asked.

"There's some disagreement among the ranks. There was a killing up there. On the surface it fits the profile, but some of the details aren't quite right," she explained. "Important details."

"He's coming, isn't he?" It was Mireya. How much she'd heard, I wasn't sure. Enough was my guess.

Ryan walked over to her and pulled her into an embrace. "We don't know. Look at me." He stepped back, tilted her chin up, and gazed into her eyes. "We'll get through this."

"Mireya, can you sense him?" Allison asked.

She shook her head. "No, but I shouldn't be able to. And last night I slept like a baby. It was the best sleep I've had in months, not a single nightmare."

Allison took a sip of her own coffee, then offered a cup to Mireya. "You've been having nightmares?"

"For a while now. I think that's why I haven't been sleeping."

"How long is a while?"

"I don't know, several weeks."

"What are the nightmares about?"

"They're...disturbing. Has something happened?" Mireya looked about the room. "Out with it," she demanded.

Allison sat down at the table. "Someone from the PSF was here a short while ago. Remember Agent Renfield?"

"Yes," Mireya replied. "Tall, dark and—"

"That's the one. He came to reinstate the shield."

"Jesus. It was down?"

"For a couple of months."

"How? Why?"

"Something to do with the death of the guy who put it in place," I told her.

"I want all of you to leave. I have this friend in San Diego. You'll be safe with him. It's far enough away. You should leave now. I can—"

"I can't leave," Ryan interrupted Allison. "What if Samuel and Dakota come back and inadvertently walk into something? I can't let anything happen to them."

"And there's no way in hell I'm leaving you here alone. I already told you that," I reminded her.

Ryan turned to Mireya. "She's right, though. You need to go."

Mireya shook her head. "You expect me to let go of the only shred of happiness I've had since... I can't even remember when?"

"When Devlin is behind bars you can come back to the ranch," Ryan reasoned.

"I'm not talking about the ranch. I'm talking about *you*. Roane will take one whiff of you and he'll know. It will take more showers and more time than we have for my scent to dissipate from you. He'll kill you, Ryan."

"Maybe so. If that's the case, your being here won't stop him. Please, Mireya."

"You're wrong. My being here will stop him. He won't hurt you. I'll see to it."

"How?"

"By agreeing to go with him."

Chapter Thirteen

I leaned on the back of the shower stall and let the water beat against my back. I didn't know which was worse, the knots in my stomach or the ones between my shoulder blades.

I'd had my fill of French toast and arguing. Like it or not, we were in this together and we were going to stand together. With luck, Dakota and Samuel would return in time and add to our numbers. If not, if Devlin struck first, then I was prepared to do what I had to, what I needed to, whatever that turned out to be.

"You've been in there for a long time."

I'd been deep in thought and hadn't even heard Allison come in.

"Are you all right?" She opened the glass shower door and steam spilled out. She was concerned about me. Maybe it was simply her nature. I wanted to believe her worry meant more.

"I'm fine."

"Liar. You can't possibly be fine."

I turned toward her and ran both of my hands through my wet hair before releasing a heavy sigh.

"You're exhausted," she said. "You need to sleep."

"There's something else I need more."

"What's that?" She leaned against the open door. She was just within my grasp. All I had to do was reach out.

"I want to hold you," I confessed.

Without hesitation she stripped off her shirt and stepped into the shower, closing the door behind her. She shut herself in there with me, in the small, confined space. The trust that conveyed meant more than I could say.

"I want you to know how sorry I am," I told her instead.

Allison placed her fingertips over my mouth. "Don't. Right now we need to be looking forward, not back."

I reached for her hand and pulled it away. "I need to say the words and you need to hear them. I may have saved you out there, but I've since put you in danger. I'm sorry. More sorry than you'll ever know."

"If it weren't for you, I wouldn't even be here."

"That may be true, but the possibility that Devlin could come tonight is eating away at me. I might not be strong enough to protect you."

"We're going to get through this."

"How do you know?"

Allison shrugged. "Because we're the good guys."

"I'm serious."

She stepped even closer. "So am I. I know you're struggling, I know you've been living a life of restraint, fighting an internal war I can't hope to understand. But I also see your goodness and your strength."

"I think—"

"Shh. Don't think." Her lips brushed softly against mine in a featherlike kiss, tentative and achingly sweet. "Just feel. Let that guard down for just a few minutes."

I closed my eyes and savored the moment. The gentleness of it, the tenderness of it was more than I deserved. She was right, of course. I'd been holding back with her, with everyone and everything. Since becoming Were I'd been living a life of half-measures, afraid to go all in, afraid if I did I would lose myself.

I inhaled deeply, breathing in the scent of her. The water cascaded over us like a warm, cleansing rain, washing away my shame. Allison's mouth followed my jaw line, then traveled down the length of my neck and across my chest. Her nails skimmed over my stomach and it knotted in anticipation. Then her fingertips trailed even lower, past my hipbone, on the way to my cock. She knew what I was and still she seemed to want me. For a moment I held my breath.

When I opened my eyes Allison was on her knees in front of me. I was long, hard and poised to enter her mouth. She wrapped her hand around me.

"You don't have to do this."

"I want to do this."

The first flick of her tongue made me shudder. I braced myself against the walls of the shower. "Christ, Allison. Don't tease me."

"You want me," she said in a hushed voice.

"Of course I do. A man would be a fool not to want you. Look at you."

She smiled, an unexpected blush rising to her cheeks.

"What would you like me to do?"

"Do?"

She leaned closer. "What is it you want, Jake?"

Everything seemed to recede into the background. There was only the two of us. The words tumbled out. "I want you to suck it."

"Yeah?"

I nodded.

"Say please?"

I grabbed a tangle of her long, dark hair and pulled back firmly. She had no choice but to look up at me. Her eyes widened and she flashed me a confident smile.

"You think you can make me beg?" I asked her. My beast liked this game. It was reminiscent of the hunt, the chase. The beast wanted to play, badly.

"Too proud to ask a girl, nicely? I'm the one on my knees."

I leaned down and kissed her, hard, my need almost painful. When I pulled away her lips were red and swollen. I soothed them with a swipe of my tongue. "Please," I begged her before rising once again to my full height. "Please."

Allison dipped a pointed tongue into the narrow slit at the tip, scooping up the drop of come oozing out.

"Mm," she moaned, wantonly licking her lips in a way that made me believe she wanted more and would take it all, every fucking drop.

"You're going to kill me," I hissed.

No sooner were the words out of my mouth, my dick was deep in hers. I bit down on my lip. Eyes closed, head back, I tried to ride the sensation. I tried to push everything else from my mind except for this moment, this feeling, this woman.

"Fuck, you're good." I was covered in spit, nice and slick. Her head was bobbing up and down, the pace fast and furious. She was hungry, devouring me, swallowing on the upstroke, building this incredible suction. She took me all the way in, right down to the root, then reached between my legs and cupped my balls.

"Jesus," I gasped, struggling to maintain control, yet at the same time wanting to lose it. "I love your mouth. Love the way your lips look wrapped around my cock. Don't stop. Don't—"

My train of thought was cut off by a new sensation. A finger, wet and slippery, had reached behind and was knocking at my back door. The cheeks of my ass flexed. Before I had time to think, Allison had pushed into the tight opening of my ass. At first it was just the tip of her finger. But as I pumped in and out, fucking her mouth, she penetrated deeper. My balls drew up, full and heavy. My legs felt weak. I was panting, light-headed. I was so close, right at the edge.

Allison moaned and I felt the vibration through my entire body, every nerve, every fiber of my being.

"Gonna come, sweetheart," I warned her, expecting her to back off.

She didn't.

Neither did I.

I shot off, releasing come into the back of her throat, again and again. Allison swallowed it down. She milked me dry, then licked me clean. I was reeling, unsteady, wanting to say something, anything, but I couldn't string together a coherent thought, never mind form words. I'd had my share of blowjobs but never, ever, anything like this.

I turned off the shower before falling to my knees. I pulled Allison to me, gathering her onto my lap where I could feel the heat of her pussy. Then I slid my hand down between us. I wanted to make her come, to take care of her the way she'd so generously taken care of me.

"Stop," she whispered, her voice tremulous as she placed her hand over mine. "Just...kiss me."

"Anything you want. Anything," I whispered as I covered her faced with soft, slow kisses. I crushed my mouth to hers, plunging my tongue inside. I could taste myself. I didn't care. I also tasted her. And she was delicious. I wanted to lick every inch of her, to drink her down, to hold her close and never let go. As the thought entered my mind, in my arms she shattered.

I waited for a minute or two before pulling back.

"You okay?"

Allison nodded. She was still trembling. I reached up and grabbed the towel I'd draped over the shower door before hopping in.

"You came." I wrapped the towel around her.

"Yeah," she replied breathlessly.

"I didn't even touch you."

Her eyes misted over with tears. She reached up and caressed the side of my face. "You touched me," she murmured, wrapping her arms around me. "Now, just hold me."

I did, I held her. And though I tried to stave it off, a deep sadness came over me. I'd just experienced one of the most joyous and connecting moments of my life. I was in love. I was certain of it. I was also certain that in the end, when she came to her senses and asked me to, I was going to have to let Allison go.

Chapter Fourteen

"Tell me about Devlin."

I carelessly dropped the towel that had been around my waist onto the floor of Mireya's room and crawled into the bed. The sheets smelled like pack and like Allison. My body relaxed as I slipped between them and pulled them over me.

"You need to sleep." Allison sat on the edge of the bed and ran her fingers through my hair in the same way my mother used to. It was soothing, comforting, familiar.

"Think of it as a bedtime story." I closed my eyes, relishing the moment.

She leaned down and kissed me on the cheek. "Bedtime stories should end with a happily-ever-after. Rest now. We'll talk when you wake up."

Before she could get up, I reached for her wrist and stopped her.

"You want me in top form. That's why you're suddenly so worried about my care and feeding. I guess Ryan's right, all women want Alpha's."

Allison frowned. "I want you alive. No offense, but physically you're no match for Devlin. You challenge his authority and he'll kill you."

"He's that much stronger than me?"

"He's that much more dangerous than you."

"Great, and you expect me to sleep?" I started to climb out of bed.

She placed her hand on my chest. "Whoa, cowboy. There's good news."

"Okay, I'll bite. What's the good news?"

"We're smarter than Devlin. Also, we're not so crazy."

"What are we going to be up against?"

Allison swallowed. I waited for her to say something, but she didn't. Not right away. Finally, she stood, moved over to the window, and pulled the curtains closed. "This is the stuff nightmares are made of. You have no idea, Jake. Besides, a lot of what I know is confidential."

"Fuck that." I rolled onto my side and leaned up. "You know what he intends to do, what he's capable of. Sharing that information could save lives. It's just you and me, darlin'. Tell me what I need to know to—"

"To stop him?" She faced me. "I'm not sure I want you to try, one misstep and... Like I said, he's strong, Jake, incredibly strong. And his strength is fueled by a maniacal obsession."

"Tell me what I need to know in order to understand him. How about we start there?"

Allison gathered her hair up and tied it into a knot on top of her head. She was wearing a pair of Mireya's scrubs. She looked tired, despite the fact that she'd slept last night.

"Now you sound like a shrink," she teased.

"Or a lawyer. You've been around enough attorneys to know a good trial lawyer doesn't directly attack the opposition's case, he systematically exploits its weaknesses."

"What if there are no weaknesses?"

She was pacing now, from the window to the bedroom door, pausing occasionally to lift back the edge of the curtain and peer outside. I flashed back to my meeting a few months ago with Byron Renfield. He was a pacer. He'd walked back and forth in front of the windows behind his desk as we'd talked, pausing occasionally to look outside. I'd had the impression he was waiting for something, watching for something. I had the same impression now.

"There are always weaknesses," I told her with more confidence than I felt.

She moved over to Mireya's dresser and reached for one of her many bottles of perfume. "Are you familiar with the Pawnee creation myth?"

"No. It's relevant?"

Allison nodded as she unscrewed the cap of the first one and took a whiff. "Very." Her nose wrinkled. She moved on quickly to the next one and seemed to like it even less. I hadn't seen her like this, restless and fidgety.

"Tell me about it."

She made her way back to the window. "According to the myth, the wolf was the first creature to experience death." Allison leaned against the wall and once again peered through the curtains. "The Pawnee were divided into four bands, one was the Skidi, or wolf. According to their legend, a great council was formed to decide how the earth would be made. All of the animals were invited, except for Sirius."

"Are we talking about the star?"

"The Wolf Star." She was pacing again, her nervous energy setting me on edge. "The council charged The Storm that Comes out of the West with making sure all was well on the earth. During the day Storm traveled the earth with a bag containing the first people. At night, when it was time to rest, he'd set down the bag and let them out to set up camp and hunt buffalo. Resentful, the Wolf Star sent a gray wolf to follow Storm."

"I sense trouble."

Allison nodded. "The wolf steals the bag. When he opens it the people come out. Only this time, there are no buffalo to hunt. Soon the people realize they were released by the wolf and not by Storm. Then, out of anger, they chase down the wolf and kill it."

"Making it the first creature to die?"

"Exactly."

"Connect the dots for me."

"Storm finds the people and he tells them to skin the wolf. The people's memory of what had happened was wrapped inside a sacred bundle made from the wolf's pelt. By killing the wolf, Storm explained, the people had brought death into the world and would henceforward be known as the Skidi, the Wolf People."

"The first Were?"

"That's what Devlin believes."

"Is Devlin Pawnee?"

"Not even close."

"But that's just a myth, right?"

"Humans have a creation story too. Various cultures have differing versions, but billions believe."

"So how does this help us understand Devlin?"

"In order to appreciate the impact learning about this had on his psyche, you have to first understand how broken it was and why."

"Okay."

"Devlin was raised in a string of foster homes in the New England area. The families he was placed with ran the gamut, everything from born-again religious types to abusive drug addicts who whored him out. When he was fifteen he ran away from home."

I propped the pillows up against the headboard behind me and leaned back. "I have a feeling things ended up going from bad to worse."

"You'd be right. He was a kid on the streets, doing what he needed to in order to get by. One rainy night he was picked up and offered a ride and a room for the night by a man in a van, he was Pawnee. Devlin had seen the guy pick up other kids before and he wasn't naïve, or so he thought. He suspected the guy was going to want something in exchange, but what that was, at fifteen and human... Devlin couldn't begin to imagine."

"The man wasn't human?"

Allison winced and I knew what was coming.

"He was Were?"

She nodded. "I'm sorry. I didn't mean..."

I held up my hand. "It's all right. Go on."

She shook her head. "No. It's not all right. It was thoughtless of me and stupid. You're human, Jake."

I looked up at the ceiling. "No, I'm not. And you're right, the sooner I accept my situation, the sooner I'll adapt. What happened between the man and Devlin?" Again, she hesitated. I shifted over and patted the empty space next to me. "I'm guessing he became Devlin's maker?"

Allison came to the bed and crawled on top of it, stretching out alongside me and resting her head on my chest. "Yes."

"But there's more to it than that."

"He was brutal, Jake. He wasn't only Devlin's maker. He was his tormentor. For years he severely abused Devlin, sexually and physically. He led by fear and domination and all that time Devlin was his whipping boy. Trapped, unable to escape."

"What happened?"

"The boy grew up."

"He got even?"

"He got deadly."

Allison sat up, her words flowing freely now.

"He snapped. Before his eighteenth birthday he was taken back to the Plains where he was passed off as the man's stepson. It was there he heard the creation myth and learned about the Morning Star ceremony."

"What's that?"

"Something most Pawnee would say doesn't happen anymore."

"Devlin took part in it?"

"He remembers being invited to smoke with the men. He remembers entering the sweat lodge and talking about the ceremony."

"Then?"

"It gets more jumbled. Undoubtedly he'd smoked more than tobacco. He told me he witnessed a sacrifice, then the Morning Star came to him in a vision."

Although I anticipated her answer, I asked the question anyway. "What kind of sacrifice?"

"A human sacrifice. It was a woman, around his age."

I shuddered. "Jesus, you think it really happened?"

"How much was real, I don't know. I can tell you, what he described happening during the ceremony was nothing compared to the death that's occurred since by Devlin's own hands."

"And the vision?"

"It happened the night of the supposed ceremony. He told me the Morning Star came to him and whispered in his ear, revealing to him the path of redemption."

"Redemption?"

"He was promised the return of immortality in exchange for the blood of the woman powerful enough to bind the most powerful."

"I don't understand."

"He's hunting former Immortals, Jake. The women he's killed have all been mated to one. The deaths reported in the news? They're the tip of the iceberg, just a small fraction of what he's responsible for. With each victim he thinks he's getting closer. With each kill he's sought out prey who are stronger, more powerful."

"Christ, no wonder Dell is worried."

"Byron and Violet Renfield have got to be high on Devlin's list."

It wasn't that many months ago I'd stood in the couple's living room. "But I thought their relationship was still a well-kept secret. How would Devlin even know?"

"His last three victims all knew the Renfields. The last two were close, personal friends. When you look at the history, it's almost as if each kill is somehow pointing Devlin to his next."

"In the news they said he was torturing them. Is that why? To get them to talk?"

"It's complicated. These murders are ritualistic. Before the victim dies, he plays with them, just like he was played with. In the end they are slaughtered, the woman's heart consumed. The former Immortal, wherever he may be, is turned to ash, a double sacrifice to the Morning Star."

My stomach lurched. Bile rose burning the back of my throat.

"All in the name of righteousness," I murmured.

"So Devlin can return to what he believes he was meant to be."

"Immortal."

"Yes."

"That's crazy."

Allison grew quiet, thoughtful.

"Come on, you don't think that's crazy?" I asked her.

"I used to think I had a good handle on things, Jake. A set of rules, a nice little manual filled with diagnoses, a sense of morals and values, of beliefs and convictions."

"And then?"

"I discovered my little corner of the world was just that, a little corner. Don't get me wrong. I've met Devlin. Without a shadow of a doubt I can tell you he's dangerous and unbalanced. What he's doing? It's completely outside the boundaries of either my society or the Were's."

"But?"

"His conviction is strong. His belief in what he's doing firmly rooted. When I was talking to him, there were moments I was almost convinced this vision, this quest he's on, is real."

"Did he confess to murdering those women?"

Allison shook her head.

"No. He's clever. He's not going to admit to killing outright. He'd say things like, 'Sometimes it's necessary to sacrifice a few for the salvation of many'."

"So, it's not just that he believes he's saving himself, he believes he's saving his people."

"Including Mireya. He thinks by taking into his own body that which was powerful enough to steal immortality, he can somehow gain it himself."

I sat there in silence. I wasn't sure what I expected, but this bizarre "you are what you eat" scenario sure as hell wasn't it.

"I told you it wasn't pretty."

"Darlin', you weren't kidding. How the hell did Mireya get involved in all of this?"

"When Devlin had the vision, he snapped. He lost control and murdered his maker. After, he returned to New England. He tracked down and systematically eliminated each and every member of his pack. The last bunch he got rid of lived together in a small den. They fought hard. He lost a lot of blood."

"So much that he couldn't shift?"

"He obviously tried, to no avail. A stranger found him early in the morning, collapsed on the sidewalk. He was naked and just a hairsbreadth from death."

"Don't tell me, Mireya was the one who found him."

"No. But when he came to at the hospital, her face was the first one he saw."

"He was her patient."

"Yes. For Devlin it was love at first sight. The Morning Star told him the woman was to be his mate. She helped save his life, then he took hers. One night he just disappeared from his room, on the same night she turned up missing."

"He kidnapped her and turned her," I said, my heart aching at the thought. "Did he...?" I felt a slight pressure behind my eyes. I closed them tight and pinched the bridge of my nose.

Allison placed her hand over mine. "Force her? Yes. She was his captive. It's amazing she survived."

"Her beast is surprisingly strong."

"It had to be. Do you suppose Devlin somehow sensed her potential?"

"No idea." I was still hopelessly ignorant about so much. I made a mental note to ask Ryan. "I can't imagine what she must have gone through. She'll martyr herself to save us."

"I know."

"I can't just stand by and let her go with him, Allison, I can't."

"You said earlier they were trying to recruit you for the Academy. Tell me more."

"Why?"

"There might be something there. Very few get invited to attend. For some reason you were. What did Renfield say when he contacted you?"

I tried to remember our initial conversation in detail, only exhaustion was taking hold. I sighed, and it turned into a yawn. "Initially we spoke by phone. The call came from out of the blue. He said he wanted to offer me an opportunity to attend some special school. I declined. I told him I was perfectly happy with the school I was going to."

"That's it?"

"He said my current school couldn't begin to teach me the things I needed to learn, to prepare me."

"Prepare you?"

"For what was to come." I yawned again. "He sent me a plane ticket. He wanted a meeting, face-to-face. I told him it would be a waste of time, that I'd just be flying up to say no in person, but he was insistent. I don't think he believed me."

I leaned my head back against the pillow and my eyes drifted shut.

"But that's what happened, you said no?"

"Yeah."

"Why did they want you? Jake?"

My eyes fluttered open. "Huh?"

"Why did they want you?"

"I wish I knew."

Did I say those words out loud or just think them? I wasn't sure. Before I could ask, I'd forgotten what the subject had even been. I couldn't hold on to my thoughts. As they slipped away into oblivion, so did I.

Chapter Fifteen

I woke with a start. The house was dark and silent. I sat up in bed, alarmed. It seemed I'd slept most of the day away. Allison was sprawled out alongside me, her hair spread across the pillow.

I slipped from between the warmth of the covers and pulled on a pair of sweats. The house was dreadfully cold. My breath caught and froze on the air. The door to the bedroom was ajar. There was a draft coming in from the hallway and I ventured toward it.

The hallway was colder, the living room colder still. The fire in the grate had gone out, the last of its embers turned to white ash. I heard the wind whipping about outside, whistling through the trees. Why had Ryan and Mireya let the fire go out? More importantly, why hadn't they wakened me?"

I crouched down in front of the hearth, intending to start it once again. Something wasn't right. A sudden, steady knocking sound drew my attention. It was coming from the kitchen.

Bang. Bang. Bang.

A chill ran up my spine, colder than the freezing temperature surrounding me. Instinct told me to run. It also told me to protect what was mine.

Bang. Bang. Bang.

I moved, cautiously toward the sound. I peered around the corner, into the kitchen. The door to the outside was wide open. With each gust of wind it flew back, hit the wall, then swung forward a few inches.

Bang. Bang. Bang.

By the light of the full moon, I could see the snow was coming down, fast and furious. It blew into the room and swirled about, a heavy dusting covered the floor and countertops. Every surface seemed thick with frost. I crossed the threshold and stepped onto the ice-cold floor. It was slippery and on the way to catch the door before it banged again, I faltered. My arms wheeled about in a futile attempt to maintain balance. I reached out for the door, grasping hold as if it were my lifeline and used it to steady myself. When I went to close it, something caught my eye. The five-point buck I'd seen the night before. It stood in the clearing, staring at me. I paused to look back, noticing for the first time that it appeared injured.

A part of me was drawn to it. My body began to warm, anticipating the change. My skin began to itch. My mouth watered. I knew it could be mine. It was almost as if the animal were calling to me, beckoning, inviting me to the slaughter. The deer's hind leg buckled and it started to go down, but it recovered. For a moment it stood tall and proud. I lifted my head and scented the air. The snow melted as it hit my bare skin. I was no longer cold. An indescribable hunger rose within me, insistent and wild. Tempting. I pushed it down. The deer wasn't the prey.

The animal looked down at the ground and my gaze followed, resting on the growing pool of blood, black against the darkness of the night in the snow. Its hind leg buckled again, first one, then the other. This time it went down. A dusting of powder billowed up into the air around it. It was the bait.

Something stirred behind me, a motion so subtle I almost missed it. Almost. I turned quickly. The door slammed, trapping me inside. I was the prey.

There was no place for me to go. No way to escape. It was Devlin, naked and newly transformed, the telltale tendrils of smoke rising up from his body, dissipating into the frigid night air. Covered in sweat, dripping with blood, he growled, baring his teeth.

The wolf inside me instinctively cowered. It was time for a show of submission. My survival depended on it. But the man before me was riveting. His green eyes were bright with purpose, singular and focused. They were level with mine and stood out in stark contrast to the long jet-black hair that fell wet and matted about and in front of his face. He matched me in height, but he was brawnier. Muscles rippled beneath his skin, poised for attack.

Time stood still. Stopped. Then all hell broke loose.

With one sure, powerful thrust he shoved me back against the door. Clawed hands ripped my chest, tearing through muscle and bone. In a violent fury, they searched for the prize. All I had time for was a sharp intake of breath. My legs buckled and I slid to the ground. A rib pierced my lung and blood started to bubble up into my throat. I wanted to shout out a warning, but I couldn't. He had my heart in his hand and he wasn't going to let go. There was nothing I could do to protect them, nothing I could do to save myself. I'd forgotten *I* was the hunter. The mistake was going to cost me, dearly. I was going to die. I'd failed them. I'd failed them all.

I woke with a start and bolted upright in bed. I lifted a shaky hand to my brow. My heart was racing. I was practically nauseous from the rush of adrenalin still coursing through my body.

"Are you all right?" Allison stepped into the room.

"Just a dream," I told her, trying desperately to put the pieces together.

"Bad one?"

I nodded. "You did warn me Devlin's story was the type of thing nightmares are made of. Perhaps I should have listened."

"You called out to me." She was holding a steaming mug in her hand. "I was in the kitchen making tea. Would you like some?" She offered me the cup, then hesitated. "I don't know if you even like tea."

I reached for the cup and took a sip.

"I like tea." The brew was warm and bitter.

"There's so much I don't know about you." She reached out and lightly brushed where the scar from Mireya's attack should have been. "There's so much I want to know."

I set the cup down on the nightstand next to the bed and gathered Allison in my arms. Pulling her in close and then turning to drop her alongside me in the bed, our faces just inches apart.

"There's a lot I'm still trying to figure out, a lot I don't know, or understand. Before the accident happened, my path was clear. Now? It's all muddled. Initially I figured with time I'd get back on track and my life would return to normal. But it's not." I paused for a moment, wrestling with the truth that for me had become perhaps the most painful. "I'm not. I'm never going to be."

"Normal?"

I nodded.

"What's it been like?" she asked quietly.

"I don't know." I rolled onto my back and stared up at the white ceiling, searching for the words to describe what I'd been going through. She was patient and finally one came.

"Lonely," I admitted. "No one knows, Allison."

"Not even your family?"

"No one. And it has to stay that way."

"Why?"

"They'd look at me differently. If people knew, my life would be over."

She leaned up on her elbow. "It would change, Jake. It wouldn't be over. The people who love you, they'd still love you."

I looked her right in the eye and laid it on the line. "Could you love me? Knowing what's inside me?"

She didn't even blink. It was almost as if she'd expected the question. Instead of answering, she asked a question of her own. "What's inside you, Jake?"

"You saw it, what I become."

"No. I see what you are. What you'll become? Neither of us knows yet and only you can decide."

"You make it sound like I have a choice."

"You do. The choices are different now. You talk about your beast as if it's separate and apart from you."

"I want it to be."

"Because?"

"There are parts of it I don't like. Parts I can't control."

She nodded. "Think back to before the accident. Did you like everything about yourself? Surely there were faults, shortcomings, a little weakness or flaw here or there?"

I smiled. "Nope. I was perfect."

She slapped me playfully on the chest. I caught her hand, brought it to my mouth and pressed a kiss on top of it. "Of course I had faults, still do."

"You've reconciled the fact that those qualities are a part of you, a part of who you are."

"You're saying the beast is a part of me too?"

Allison surprised me. With a growl of frustration she pounced, pinned my hands over my head and straddled my hips. "Listen to me!"

"I am listening."

"You're still talking in absolutes. The man. The beast. You are *Were*. Sometimes you hide it, sometimes you don't. Sometimes you want to and can't. But it's what you are."

"Do you believe in fate?"

"I don't know."

"Dell said he didn't believe in coincidences," I continued. "What do you suppose he meant? Do you think somehow I was meant to find you?"

"Why do they want you at the Academy?" Again asked a question instead of supplying me with an answer.

"Dell said his father thinks I'm important. Something about an intuition."

"An Intuitive?"

"Yeah. She saw something. What? I don't know and he didn't say. Whatever it was, Renfield thinks it's about me."

Allison appeared to mull over the possibilities. "Promise me something?"

"What?"

"If Devlin comes tonight, no matter what else happens, survive, endure. Even if you have to run away."

"You want me to run?"

"Yes. I want you to run. Do you hear me, Jake?"

I placed my hand over hers and gave it a gentle squeeze. "Darlin', I've never run away from a fight before. I'm not about to start now. I didn't save you just to let you go. I didn't save you to abandon you."

Allison leaned down and pressed her lips to mine in an almost chaste kiss. When she pulled away her eyes were filled with tears.

"Maybe this isn't about you saving me. Maybe this is about me saving you. Have you thought of that?"

I rolled my eyes then flipped her over. She separated her legs and I lowered my hips between them.

"I'm gonna ask you one more time, and this time you're going to give me a straight answer. Could you love me? Knowing what's inside me?"

"I think I already do."

Allison wasn't the first woman to tell me she'd loved me. There were a few in high school and one my freshman year of college. None of whom I'd ever said it back to. None of whom I'd felt that way about. Did I push her into saying it? Maybe I did. If so, I shouldn't have, plain and simple.

I knew she had baggage. She was just getting over a bad marriage. Why did I do it when there was nothing I could offer her? Because in the space of a few days I'd fallen for her and, although normally I'd loathe admitting it, I needed the assurance that she felt the same way about me. I'd needed it just like I'd needed her, desperately. Did I fess up? Did I tell her? No.

Why? Because I was afraid if I said the words, she'd try to stop me from doing what I needed to do. Instead I kissed her, passionately, deeply, letting the emotions I dared not verbally express spill into her mouth. She moaned and writhed beneath me as I ground against her pussy and palmed her breast.

She returned my sense of urgency in a way that was almost heady. One second her hands were in my hair, the very next they were tugging at the blankets trapped between us. I broke off the kiss and arched up. Allison pulled down the covers.

"Want you," she gasped.

My cock was long and hard, between us. She moved to reach for it. I grabbed hold of her wrist. "No!" I stretched her arm up over her head.

Allison smiled, undeterred. She reached down with her other hand. I was faster.

"I said no." Now I had both of her arms trapped, one hand holding both of her wrists in place. There was a press of something, a stirring from within. I closed my eyes and began to turn away.

"Stay with me, Jake!"

I could feel the beast, inside. Pacing. Panting. It wanted Allison as much as I did. Maybe even more. I released her wrists. "I'm trying."

She grabbed hold of my chin. "No, you're hiding. You're pulling away. Why?"

"You..."

"I what?"

"You excite me."

She brazenly reached for my cock. "I noticed."

My muscles tensed. I thought about pulling back but then she leaned up and licked me. Her tongue swept up over my throat from the hollow of my neck to the tip of my chin.

"Mmm," she moaned.

I pushed her back down, pinning her to the mattress. "You excite *all* of me." I whispered my confession into the shell of her ear and she trembled beneath me. "You have no idea how much."

Her heart was pounding, louder, faster. Her thumb ran over the tip of my cock. She wet her lips as she spread the oozing pre-come over its head. "Tell me."

"You seem to awaken something, to call to something deep inside me." My voice sounded deeper, more gravelly than it normally did. Was it emotional need? Physical arousal? Or, was it something else?

Allison's breath hitched, her body tensed. She was aroused, but she was also afraid. And she should have been. I should have been too. I wasn't. Somehow, by making the admission, in embracing the truth, I'd discovered a balance. I moved slowly down her body, scenting every inch of her. I lifted up the shirt she was wearing and nuzzled between her breasts before venturing lower.

"You smell amazing." The aroma was intoxicating. Her desire for me leaked from every pore. I hooked my fingers in the waistband of the scrubs and lowered them. "You want me."

"Yes."

I tossed the pants behind me, then spread her legs wide and lowered myself between them. "I have to taste you. Suck you. Fuck you," I murmured, almost to myself as I separated the lips of her pussy with my fingers. She was already slick, her cunt glistening, its flesh a deep ripe red. I flattened my tongue and began to feast, lapping up her warm juices as they flowed out of her and into my mouth. I explored every contour, every crevice, luxuriating in the sounds I was coaxing from her, in the desire dripping from her.

Allison laced her hands through my hair and arched up. I let my tongue unfurl and slip inside, reaching further, going deeper than I'd ever been able to before, probing, swirling. Allison cried out.

"Jake!"

I pulled back and gazed up at her. "I want to please you. I want to make you come like you've never come before."

Her eyes widened.

"What is it?" I asked.

"Your eyes, they're blue."

"The better to see you with, my dear."

I didn't blink. I didn't look away. I kept my gaze locked on hers.

A slow smile graced her lips. The second it did, I slid back down toward my target.

I latched onto her clit, pulling it into my mouth and worrying it gently between my teeth, flicking it with my tongue. I slid two fingers into her empty cunt.

"More!" she gasped.

Who was I to argue? I slipped in a third. Sliding them in and out as I sucked. Within seconds my fingers were well coated, her body close to orgasm. Allison's body was primed. My eyes landed on the puckered hole of her ass. I remembered how it had felt when she'd touched me there. Tentatively, I slid my thumb toward it.

"How much more do you want?" I asked, pushing my thumb lightly against the center before tracing the outward edges.

"I don't know," she whispered.

Maybe she didn't, but her body did. Her cream was flowing freely, I spread it down and around. Teasing. Testing. I wanted more of it, more of her. I wanted to see her completely undone and I wanted to be the cause of it. I knew what it was like to have something so thoroughly, so profoundly inside you that you couldn't tell where you stopped and where it started. I wanted to be that something, to be that intensely connected to her.

My tongue pierced her pussy once again and at the same time I slid the tip of my thumb into her ass. The instant I did, she went. The muscles in her ass clamped down, her vaginal walls fluttered, involuntarily tightening. I let her ride the sensation for a few seconds. Then I started moving once again, fucking her with my long, thick tongue in a way she was certain to later dream about, to forever crave. My thumb went in further, pushing past the tight ring to massage the flesh inside, stretching it.

"Please, Jake."

She was panting now, like a bitch in heat. My cock was throbbing. I withdrew my mouth from her cunt long enough to spit on my hand.

It was her turn to beg. "Please what?"

She was fisting the bed sheets as I replaced the thumb with two fingers, probing further, loosening her. Her head was thrown back. Her body expectantly bowed. She was on the edge once again. This time, so was I.

"Fuck me."

I love it when a girl talks dirty. "Do you kiss your momma with that mouth?"

"I sucked your dick with it earlier today," she saucily replied.

"And you did a damn fine job, too. That's why I'm rewarding you." I rolled her clit between my thumb and forefinger and watched her go again. This time she came even harder. I didn't wait for the calm. I moved up her body and covered it with mine. My lips hungrily sought hers, and then I entered her, with one, sure thrust.

I felt the need to move, but I held fast. Buried to the hilt, I swallowed her screams in a demanding kiss, taking possession of her mouth. She seized hold of my upper arms, her nails dug into my biceps. When I broke off the kiss, she was still trembling beneath me, eyes closed. I leaned up on my forearms so I could see her face.

"Look at me, Allison." I eased out, then slid back in using long, luxurious strokes.

Her eyes opened and locked on mine.

"You okay?" I asked, keeping the pace slow and even. "You still with me, baby?"

Allison smiled. "I'm still with you."

"Good. This..." I rotated my hip on the downstroke so that my cock dragged against her clit. I leaned down and kissed along the length of her jaw line back to just below her ear. I was holding on by a mere thread. My stomach was a mass of coils, my balls tight and heavy. "This isn't me fucking you."

Her calves traveled up over the backs of mine. She wrapped her legs around me, her arms around me and held on. I held on too. I tried to focus on the sound of Allison's breathing and the steady creaking of the mattress beneath us.

"What is this?"

"This..." I was on the precipice. I felt a brush of fur. The cage door few open. I was running. The wind rushed past me as I raced closer and closer to the brink. I thrust in once more. "This..." Twice more. Her nails scraped my back. She cried out in pleasure, exploding around me. I flew off the edge, letting go and coming hard, so hard it was almost dizzying. "...is me making love to you," I whispered, earnestly, into the shell of her ear.

I'd poured myself into satisfying her, working her with my hands and mouth and cock. Somehow it still didn't seem enough.

I rolled off her, then gathered her into my arms. I let my hands wander over her back, stroking it possessively, soothing her. "I've fucked a lot of women. But I've never made love to one before."

Allison lifted her head. "What's the difference, Dallas?"

"The love part?" I swallowed down the lump in my throat. "I'm afraid when it comes to stuff like this, I'm not very eloquent. I'm a man of few words."

"It's only three."

"I love you."

She kissed me, tenderly, on the mouth. "I love you, too."

Chapter Sixteen

After our declaration of love, Allison had dozed off and was still napping. Sleep was the furthest thing from my mind. Every muscle, every fiber of my being was on alert. There had been no sign of Samuel and Dakota. Darkness would be falling in just a few hours.

Mireya joined me at the window. "Checking out your handiwork? That's some army you built out there."

I nodded. "Was bored. Couldn't sleep." I took a sip of the tea I'd just made. "Where's Ryan?"

"Entertaining Wright. They're playing a board game. Where's Allison?"

"Resting."

"The snow's still coming down awfully hard. Do you think the bad weather will work for us, or against us?"

"I don't know." I turned to face her. "Is he coming?"

"I don't know."

I wanted to believe her, but I didn't.

"You had a sense before the shields went back up, a feeling." She turned to walk away, but I reached out and stopped her. "You mentioned having dreams."

"Nightmares. Yes."

"Tell me about them."

"They weren't clear, Jake."

"You must remember something."

She shrugged. "Only bits and pieces, impressions mostly."

"Impressions of what?"

"Places, people...hunger. When I thought the shields were in place, I dismissed them. But now? I'm not so sure."

"You probably know Devlin better than anyone. Do you think it's possible for him to track you?"

"Without the shields, I'm sure of it. He's done it before."

"Tell me about it."

She pulled away. "I don't like to talk about it."

I wasn't going to take no for an answer. "Well, you're going to have to talk about it."

She glared at me, defiantly, but I held firm. I couldn't back down. There was too much at risk.

"You stepping up to the plate?" she asked, a little too snidely for my taste.

I reminded myself that posturing was part of the game and it was a game I'd seen Mireya play well. "Like it or not, right now I'm the strongest male." I lowered my voice. "And, I'm willing to bet I'm the strongest wolf."

She held my gaze. "You didn't fare so well earlier."

I moved in just a tad closer. "They say practice makes perfect. There are people in this house who I care about, who I love. I intend to protect them."

"There are people in this house that I love too. You, Wright, Allison, you're no threat to Roane."

"I notice you didn't say Ryan."

"If I handle things just right, it won't be a problem."

"You seriously think Devlin's the kind of Alpha that's going to tolerate another wolf coming in his bitch?"

Mireya winced.

"No. Fucking. Way," I said. "This isn't going to end easily and you know it."

"Stay out of this. I beg of you. When he shows up, just...stand down."

"When. You said when. He's coming."

"No matter how far I run, he always manages to track me down and bring me back." Mireya released a tired sigh. "This time, it's just taking him longer."

"How long does it usually take?"

She involuntarily shivered. "The first time, it took him just a few days."

"Then you turned right around and ran again?"

"Not right away. I had to...recover."

"He hurt you."

"Roane thought of it as teaching me a valuable lesson. Ironically it did teach me something. It taught me to plan better. Unfortunately, the plan still wasn't good enough."

"He found you that time too?"

"In a couple weeks. The third time it took him almost a month. I finally realized I was kidding myself. The truth was I couldn't run from Roane any more than I could run from myself."

"I don't understand."

"We're mated, Jake. For good or bad, we're bound to one another. It doesn't matter where I go, what I do. Given enough time he'll find me, and he'll drag me back."

I wrapped my arm around her shoulders. "Not this time. We won't let him."

"I wish I believed that. But I don't. He's probably out there now, watching, waiting, biding his time." Mireya gazed out the window, her expression resigned. "For a man like him, the hunt isn't something you do out of necessity to satisfy the beast, it's not a pastime or a hobby, it's an art form. He considers it sacred, beautiful, in service of a higher purpose. No one does it better."

"You're not alone. You were those other times, but you aren't now."

"We need to get something straight." She stepped back and faced me head-on. "If Devlin comes, he isn't going to leave without me. I don't want you to get hurt. I don't want any of you to get hurt."

"And you've been hurt enough. You've suffered enough. You deserve to have your life back. You deserve the chance to move on, to be happy. Ryan loves you, you know. He wants a life with you," I told her.

She shook her head. "This isn't going to end happily-ever-after for me, Jake."

"It might."

"How?"

"I haven't quite figured that out yet," I admitted. "I will, though."

Mireya patted me on the shoulder. "Well, you just keep on thinking, college boy. When you come up with a plan, you let me know."

"And you'll poke holes in it."

"Probably."

"Meanwhile, how about you poke some holes in Devlin's?"

"What do you mean?"

I walked over to the sofa and sat down. Mireya followed.

"Where is he gonna go wrong? Where is he vulnerable? Think. What do you know about him that could be helpful?"

She lowered her head and tiredly rubbed her temples. "I honestly don't know. I've spent most of the past year trying to forget Roane Devlin."

"Jake? I think I'd like some tea. Would you mind?"

It was Allison. She was fresh from the shower, the aroma of soap still clinging to her skin. I stood, she walked into my open arms and I gathered her to my chest in a comforting embrace.

"Did you have a nice nap?" I placed a kiss on top of her head.

She nodded. "Is the power back on?"

"No. We're still running on the generator."

"How are you holding up?" Allison asked Mireya, taking the seat I'd previously occupied.

"A hell of a lot better than the last time you asked me that question."

Allison placed her hand over Mireya's. "You've been through a lot."

"I want to put all this behind me."

"You will," Allison assured her.

"As long as Roane is alive I'm connected to him. I can deny it, try to mask it, shield against it..."

"But it's there," finished Allison.

Mireya nodded. "I'm afraid I'm never going to get my life back."

"Unless we take his." Ryan was leaning against the doorjamb, a dishtowel thrown casually over one shoulder, hands buried deep in the pockets of his blue jeans.

"You are not going up against Roane. If you do, he'll kill you," Mireya replied with a frankness that made me cringe.

Ryan dried his hands on the towel. "I might surprise you."

"If he agrees to a bake-off, you'll be the first guy I call."

"I deserve better from you," Ryan said quietly, standing his ground. "I'm going to let the insult slide because I know you're under a lot of stress."

Before Mireya could respond, he turned and walked away.

"Shit! I wasn't trying to hurt his feelings."

"What *were* you trying to do, Mireya?" Allison asked.

"Rip out his balls?" I suggested, making no attempt to hide my anger.

"No! I'm trying to protect him." Mireya insisted, climbing to her feet. She wanted to go after him. Whether to apologize or further press her point, I couldn't tell.

"Wait." I moved in front of her.

"I need to explain."

"You need to apologize," I told her.

"What I said is true, Jake."

"Probably, but you should have said it differently."

"I will. I've got to make him understand."

"Just not right now. Give him a little space. You know Ryan, he never stays mad for long. By the time dinner rolls around he'll have forgiven you."

"What if he hasn't?"

"He will," Allison assured her.

I didn't stick around long enough to hear Mireya's reply. At the moment, I was more concerned about Ryan.

"Can you believe her?" Ryan growled. He was standing at the island in the kitchen, mercilessly pounding out a chicken breast with a meat tenderizer.

"It's like you said, she's under a lot of stress. We all are. She took it out on you. You're taking in out on the chicken."

He paused mid-swing and set the mallet down. Ryan was a peacemaker, a nurturer. Anger and aggression were relatively foreign to him. He shook it off, quickly. "I don't want to lose her, Jake."

"I know."

"I'll fight for her if I have to." He made the statement with heartfelt conviction.

I hopped up onto the counter and braced myself. The next part was going to be painful.

"Don't take this the wrong way, okay?" I asked before saying what needed to be said. "If you fight for her, you'll lose."

"Thanks for the vote of confidence."

"Come on, Ryan. We're talking about Roane Devlin. Like it or not, you and I both know that man's got a healthy dose of crazy in his can of whoop ass. Devlin's bigger than you, meaner than you, and he's ruthless."

"You almost sound like you're talking from experience," Ryan said.

I flashed back on my dream. The look in Devlin's eyes, the expression on his face as he reached inside me.

"Jake?"

"I've been listening to the girls."

"And?"

"I think Mireya's right. I hate to admit it, but I think if it comes down to a fight, he'll kill us. And I bet he doesn't even break a sweat."

"So what are you suggesting? We just hand Mireya over? We let him win?"

"We let him think he's won. We outsmart him. We dangle what he wants in front of him. We wait for an opening. Then we strike."

"How?"

"I'm going to teach you how to shoot."

"A gun? Maybe you should teach Allison or Mireya."

I shook my head. "Mireya's already willing to go with him, Ryan. She's willing to sacrifice herself to ensure our safety. Allison's tough, but she's not a killer. And if she thinks she might hit me or anyone else, she'll hesitate. I need someone who won't hesitate, someone who will do what's necessary to ensure Mireya, Allison and Wright are safe. That someone needs to be you."

"I don't know, Jake."

"Promise me."

"We've been through this. A bullet won't stop him."

"No. Not unless it's well placed. Promise me."

"I promise."

Chapter Seventeen

The sun went down. The moon rose and was full. Energy coursed through me, making my skin prickle and setting me on edge. I was itching to transform and found myself wondering if it was taking more energy to resist changing than to simply give in and do it. There was still no sign of the others.

If Devlin were traveling outside in this weather, he'd almost assuredly be doing it as a wolf. But I was fairly certain he wouldn't make his move in that form. He'd want the advantages his human body would give him. I would.

I slid another round of ammunition into the magazine, then looked up to check on Ryan.

"Open up your stance," I told him.

He adjusted his footing.

"And breathe." I added. "You're holding your breath. Relax."

"I can't relax."

"It's hard to relax when you aren't breathing."

"It's hard to relax with a gun in your hands." Ryan set the rifle down. He checked his watch. "It's freezing out here and the *cacciatore* should be close to done. We should go inside and check it."

"You said it wouldn't be ready for another hour. Besides, the girls promised they'd keep an eye on it."

"Can Allison cook? Mireya can't, that's for damn sure. It'll be ruined."

Dinner being ruined was the last thing on my mind at the moment. "Hit the target once, then we'll go in."

"Jake, I haven't even gotten close to hitting it."

"I know you can do it."

"Maybe we should try a bigger target?"

"You just need more practice. Think of the weapon as an extension of your body. Take a deep breath, relax."

I watched as Ryan reached once again for the rifle and lifted it, pressing the butt into his shoulder. He inhaled deeply, closed his eyes and slowly exhaled.

"Good. Now open your eyes, adjust the site and—"

Ryan took aim and lined up the shot. Just as he was about to squeeze the trigger a piercing cry cut through the silence of the night. Whether it was Allison or Mireya I didn't know. I didn't care.

I reached for the rifle at my side, slid home the magazine I'd just filled and took off at a run.

"Mireya?"

"I'm on my way to the kitchen," she replied. *"It was Allison."*

The snow-covered landscape flew by in a blur. I covered the distance between the barn and the house in a matter of seconds.

The door leading to the kitchen was wide open. I should have slowed down, taken heed, approached cautiously. But I didn't stop to think of that. I raced inside throwing caution to the wind.

I quickly surveyed the room. The glass from the door had shattered and was strewn about the floor. Everything else seemed in order. Allison was standing over by the island, her hand over her heart. It took Ryan a few seconds to catch up to me. Mireya ran into the kitchen just as he did, approaching from somewhere within the house.

"What happened?" I asked, my voice sounding gravely to my own ears. The promise of a hunt had awakened my beast. Fueled by the extra adrenalin, it paced back and forth inside the cage of my body, longing to break free. The muscles beneath my skin rippled. I felt a brush of fur, but I pushed it aside.

"I think it was just a gust of wind. My back was to the door, I was about to start setting the table—"

I made my way over to her, glass crunching under my feet. I placed the gun onto the counter and gathered her into my arms. Allison's heart was pounding.

"You all right?"

"Fine. Just startled." She looked at the rifle I'd put down, then at Ryan, who stood behind me carrying a second one.

Mireya noticed too. "Please tell me you aren't counting on that to stop him."

Ryan turned on the safety, before setting the rifle on top of the antique pie safe. "I've learned the hard way not to count on anything," he replied quietly before closing the kitchen door.

"Ryan—" Mireya stepped forward.

He cut her off. "There's a broom in the pantry. We need to sweep up the glass, board up the window."

"I'll get the broom," Allison offered, stepping out of my embrace.

"There's some plywood in the barn. It might do the trick," I volunteered, thinking I might ask Allison to come out to help me fetch it.

There was a pot, slowly simmering on the stove. Ryan silently gave it a stir.

"Dinner smells good." Mireya stepped closer to him, her approach uncharacteristically tenuous. She closed her eyes and inhaled. When she opened them again they were filled with a vulnerability I'd rarely seen from her.

I'd witnessed Mireya being nurturing and caring countless times. But I was always left with the impression she was holding something back, keeping her distance. Now I understood why.

"I'm sorry I hurt you earlier," she admitted, laying her hand on Ryan's bicep in a way that was familiar, yet not overly intimate. She was being cautious.

"How about you two cover the window with a trash bag and duct tape for now?" I pulled Allison's coat off the hook by the door. When she emerged from the pantry, broom in hand, I held it out to her. "I could use an extra pair of hands if you don't mind."

I nodded at Ryan and Mireya.

"Of course."

Allison handed the broom to Mireya, then turned around and let me help her on with her coat. She buttoned it up quickly while stepping into her boots. We made a hasty departure, leaving the light and warmth of the house behind to trudge out into the snow.

"Hey, Captain Obvious, wait up!" Allison was a few steps behind me when she called out.

I paused and turned. "I thought I was being subtle."

"I don't think it's possible for a Texan to be subtle."

"Ha. Ha." I leaned down, scooped her up and threw her over my shoulder.

A squeal of surprise was followed by laughter. "Put me down!" Allison demanded half-heartedly, swatting me playfully on the ass.

"I'll put you down when I'm good and ready," I told her, continuing on my way back to the barn where Ryan and I had been practicing earlier.

"I'm serious!"

"Seriously crazy about me, I know." With my free hand I pulled the door open, then stepped inside out of the wind.

"Jake!"

I encircled her waist with my hands and lifted her into the air before moving in nice and close, pinning her against the wall with my body.

"I'm in charge, here. And I said I'll put you down when I'm good and ready."

"Oh yeah?" she taunted, licking her lips and squirming against me.

"Yeah."

"Are you?"

"What?"

"Good and ready?" Allison wrapped her legs around my waist, her coat rising up. She pressed into me.

"You tell me, darlin'."

She had to have felt how aroused I was, how much I wanted her again, needed her again. I leaned in, nuzzling her neck, nibbling just behind her ear.

"Best I ever had," she whispered.

I wanted to be rid of the layers of clothes, to be surrounded by her, to bury myself deep inside her. My body ran hot. Since becoming Were, I was more tolerant of the cold. I wondered briefly if I could give off enough heat to keep us both cozy. But I dismissed the idea. It was dark now. The moon was full. I needed to keep my head on straight. As tempting as Allison was, another round with her was going to have to wait until morning.

I pulled back, then lifted one hand up to caress the side of her face. "You've been so accepting, so open. You're amazing." Allison blushed. "No more lies between us, not ever."

Her legs slid down until her feet touched the ground, the playful mood suddenly broken. "Don't make me promises, Jake."

"I'm a man of my word."

She wrapped her arms around her stomach. She was shivering in the cold, but I resisted the urge to warm her.

"Out with it." I didn't want to have this conversation. I especially didn't want to have it now. But whatever was weighing on her mind, it needed to be said.

"You're a man with good intentions. I believe that."

"My grandmother used to say the road to hell is paved with those," I told her.

"It sounds like your grandmother was a wise woman."

"About some things." I searched for a piece of plywood about the right size to place over the broken window.

"A broken heart isn't mended as easily as a broken window," she said.

"I know that." My eyes landed on a board just the right size. I set it on top of the workbench, then searched for a hammer and some nails.

"I can't afford..."

The jar of nails went into my coat pocket. The hammer I offered to Allison. She reached out for it, but I didn't let go. Her eyes sought out mine.

"I have to be careful," she finished.

"I wish I could assure you I'd never hurt or disappoint you, but I can't. That's the truth," I said.

She looked away and nodded. "I know."

I released my hold and stepped back. "When I came here to learn about what I've become, the last thing I expected to find was you."

"I didn't expect this either. I came to shed the remnants of my last relationship, not to start a new one."

"So what now? We wait for the weather to clear, collect your car, kiss goodbye, and go our separate ways? Is that what you want?"

"Is it what *you* want?"

Before I could reply a shot rang out from the direction of the house.

"What—"

"Wait here." I was out the door and halfway back to the house before I tried to communicate with Ryan and Mireya. My call went unanswered. Whatever was happening in the house, it wasn't good.

I couldn't see inside as I approached. The door was locked, the window covered with green plastic. But I could smell the blood. My pack was inside and they were in danger. On impulse I threw my shoulder against the solid wood. The frame splintered with a resounding crack. The door swung open and I crashed through it, like a bull in a china shop. Then I came to a screeching halt. My nightmare had come true. It was Devlin.

Chapter Eighteen

I couldn't see his face, because his back was to me, but I knew it was him. It had to be. He was nude. His body was slick with sweat, his muscles were pumped and bulging. Blood dripped from his shoulder. He'd been shot, but the wound didn't seem to be slowing him down, not one bit. He had Ryan pinned to the wall, rifle under his neck, feet dangling just inches above the ground. Perhaps more disconcerting was that my entrance hadn't even made him flinch. I wasn't worth so much as a glance.

"Control him, Miranda," Devlin growled. "Control him like you did the kid or I'll take this one's head clean off."

Wright was crouched down in the corner, arms protectively crossed over his head. The scent of urine hit my nostrils, Wright had wet himself. He was terrified. I couldn't blame him. Mireya stood between Devlin and me. She looked pale, afraid.

"You don't want that. Do you, my love?" Devlin taunted.

I placed my hand on top of Wright's head. He'd been rocking to and fro at a frenzied pace. My touch brought him back and he sprang up, wrapping his arms around my waist and burrowing his head in my stomach, his heart pounding.

Mireya approached Devlin. "You know I don't. Please," she begged. "You're hurt, Roane. Let me take care of your wound."

He looked back at her over his shoulder. For the first time I gazed upon his face. His features were sharp and angular, his skin pale, his eyes wide with a wildness I'd seen only in my dream. He reeked of blood and death and something else I couldn't name.

"You'd say anything right now to save him, wouldn't you?" he spat. "You'd *do* anything right now."

A chill ran down my spine. I was fairly certain whatever Devlin had in mind, it was beyond the darkest of my nightmares.

"Yes," she whispered, shoulders sagging in a way that echoed defeat. "He's no threat to you."

Roane stepped back, releasing Ryan, who crumpled to the floor, sputtering and gasping for breath.

I gave Wright's shoulder what I hoped was a reassuring squeeze. Somehow, Mireya had won the first round.

"Your scent is all over him," Devlin observed quietly, his tone suddenly and eerily devoid of passion.

"He's pack."

Devlin smiled at her. "He's your lover." He opened the bolt of the rifle and ejected the spent cartridge onto the floor. "And we both know it."

I held my breath. Every muscle in my body was tensed and ready. I swept Wright behind me and bent my knees slightly. The movement must have telegraphed my intention. Mireya caught it and spared me a look of warning. I stood stock still, expecting Devlin to chamber the next round. The next few seconds seemed like hours. Fear hung cloyingly in the air.

"I should kill you for what you've done," he hissed, towering over Ryan. Fury rolling off him in waves that made my wolf cower.

"But you won't."

It was Allison, she'd reached the doorway.

"And why not, Doctor?" Devlin placed his foot squarely on Ryan's chest, then turned to her.

If he was surprised to see her, he hid it well. I stepped to the left in front of Allison, trying to shield both her and Wright as best I could with my body. The door was still open. I willed them to turn, run, escape. Maybe between the three of us, we could hold Devlin back long enough to give them a head start. But then what?

"A gallant gesture," Devlin observed. "But the dear doctor won't run. Will you?"

"No," she agreed.

"I fascinate her," he declared proudly. He pulled the magazine out of the rifle and tossed the gun aside. "Well? Enlighten us, Doctor. Why should I let this one live?"

"Killing him would serve no purpose," Allison stated matter-of-factly.

The strained mood in the room built into a silent storm as we waited and watched. Ever so slowly the tension left Devlin's face. Only to be replaced with an equally disturbing sardonic smirk.

"It would make me feel good," he finally replied.

Much to my dismay, Allison stepped around me, exposing herself. I resisted the urge to reach for her, to pull her back. I couldn't do it and still shield Wright. Instead, I watched with rapt attention as she casually, yet deliberately, walked over to the table, pulled out a chair and sat.

"You don't kill to feel good," Allison said.

"No?"

"No." She tapped her fingers on the table. "It's not why you came. It's not part of the plan. Killing Ryan will gain you nothing. Showing mercy, on the other hand, sparing his life?"

She looked pointedly at Mireya, before finishing, "*That* will gain you something very precious to you."

Mireya picked up the cue and ran with it. "You're bleeding, Roane. You're hurt." She reached out to examine the wound, her hand noticeably trembling.

Devlin grabbed hold of her wrist, preventing her from touching him.

"I don't need your help," he said, almost absently stepping away from Ryan. He looked down at his shoulder.

I watched in amazement as the skin around the injury rippled. It happened so fast I found myself wondering if I'd imagined it. A burst of fur. An instant later skin, smooth and unmarred. The only indication left of the earlier wound was the remnants of dried blood which both streaked his torso and spattered the wall behind him.

I'd never seen or heard of a Were who could do what Devlin just had. One look at Mireya's face told me this was new for her too. I'd seen Were transform and heal themselves, but not like this, not a wound in isolation.

"How?" Mireya asked.

Devlin's eyes shown bright with a knowing power, whether real, imagined, or outright delusional I didn't know. But the mere thought that he might somehow be close to achieving what he'd set out to scared the hell out of me.

"You see?" He encircled her waist with his arm, sweeping her to him. "You see what's happening?" His hand was tangled in her hair. He'd pulled her head back. She had no choice but to look up into his eyes. "I'm close. So very close."

"I see," Mireya replied, nodding. "I see."

Ryan started to climb to his feet. Devlin moved with lightning speed. One second he had Mireya in his embrace, in the next he was on the floor, his knee planted firmly in Ryan's chest, his hand clenched around Ryan's throat, squeezing.

Without thought, I attacked. Covering Devlin's body with my own I slid one arm around his neck in a chokehold. Devlin moved with unsurpassed speed, leaning in, then turning, twisting, he threw me off. It was as if I were no more than a fly, an annoyance to be brushed off. I sailed through the air and landed hard, hitting my head on the edge of the island, the wind knocked out of me.

"Jake!" Allison was at my side. The expression on her face told me she was alarmed.

"Are you all right?"

I leaned up and gingerly touched the back of my head. When I checked my fingertips, they were smeared with blood. I nodded.

"That was stupid," she declared.

"Yes, it was," Devlin agreed. "Get the boy some ice, Miranda."

She moved over to the freezer.

"And you—" I watched from a distance as he deadlifted Ryan up off the floor by the front of his shirt. "Find me some clothes and get me something to eat. I'm hungry."

Within the space of a few minutes, the hierarchy had been established. Devlin was top dog and nobody else was even fucking close.

"What's your name, son?" he asked Wright.

Mireya answered for him. "He's just a kid, Roane."

"I was a kid once, for about five minutes. Then I had to grow up fast."

She handed me the bag of ice and Allison helped me climb to my feet. The room blurred and the earth shifted unexpectedly beneath me. I was momentarily overcome by a wave of nausea. I closed my eyes until the feeling passed. Luckily it did, and quickly.

"My name's Wright." I could see him clearly now. He'd risen to his feet and was standing tall, despite the dark stain marring the front of his blue jeans.

"Where is your maker?"

"Long gone. I live here now."

Devlin leaned down until he was eye-level with Wright. "And who is in charge here?" he asked.

Wright swallowed. "You are, sir."

The answer earned him a manly pat on the back. "Smart kid. Go shower and change your clothes."

Wright dashed from the room. If he were as smart as I thought he was, he'd change more than his pants. The weather was still horrible and whether he could find his way in to town to get help I didn't know. I was about to try to silently suggest it when Devlin caught my eye.

He looked pointedly at me. "You could learn a thing or two from him, Jake."

Ryan returned with a handful of clothes, sparing me from having to respond.

Devlin started to dress. Had he sensed my intentions? I couldn't tell. "You're a long way from home, Doctor."

"I came to the area on vacation. I was heading to a resort north of here when the storm blew in making the roads impassable. Jake rescued me."

"Did he now?" He tucked himself inside the pair of blue jeans, then reached for the zipper. Whether they belonged to Samuel or Dakota, I wasn't sure. "You expect me to believe your presence here is a coincidence?" he asked.

Allison averted her gaze. She'd faced him head-on earlier, despite the nakedness. Perhaps the act of dressing seemed more intimate to her; it did to me.

"Finding Miranda here was a surprise. You? Even more so. But a coincidence? I don't believe in those anymore, especially where you're concerned."

"You've come a long way, Doctor."

"I admit I doubted, but having seen what you can do, the power you've gained..."

"You haven't seen the half of it."

"Tell me, why am I here, Roane?" she asked.

"It's all part of the plan," he answered. "Now that you've seen with your own eyes. You can help spread the word."

He slid his feet inside a pair of fleece-lined boots that had been sitting by the door and tested the fit. Seemingly satisfied, he pulled the sweatshirt he'd been given over his head, then joined Allison at the table.

"Spread the word about what?" I asked.

Devlin looked at me, his stare cold and apprising.

"Roane?" Allison's heart rate increased. Devlin's scrutiny of me made her nervous. Hell, it made me nervous.

He turned back to Allison and smiled. "Your boy speaks."

She shrugged. "One of his many talents."

"It's nice to see you've moved on, Doctor."

"Who said I've moved on?"

Devlin rolled his eyes. "You don't have to say anything." He pointed to his nose. "He's marked you from head to toe. You're not the kind of woman to screw around. And, speaking of screwing around..." Devlin held his hand out to Mireya. "Come."

Ryan reached for her arm.

"Let me go." Tears filled her eyes. She looked from Ryan to me, silently pleading. For what? I wasn't sure.

I'd had a taste of Devlin's strength, neither Ryan nor I were going to be a match for him. That I knew. I placed my hand on Ryan's shoulder and gave it a squeeze. "Let her go," I whispered.

"Jake—" He looked stricken.

"Let her go to her mate. It was you who taught me about what it means to be mated. Remember? She has no choice. It's done."

Ryan wouldn't let go. "There's *always* a choice."

Mireya gave him a watery smile. "And I've made mine."

"I can't let you go," he managed to choke out. "I can't."

Mireya stepped closer to him, placed her hand over his wrist, and shook him off. "You never had me," she told him before turning away and breaking his heart.

"Tend to the dinner," Devlin commanded. Ryan glared at him. For a minute I thought he was going to say or do something foolish. "It's what you were doing before I arrived, yes?"

"Yes," Ryan replied as he gave the pot a stir. "It's ready. I just need to make the salad and warm up the bread."

"Good. I'm hungry, starving." Devlin pulled Mireya down onto his lap. "It's been ages since I've been...satisfied." He wrapped a tendril of her hair around his finger, drawing her in, slowly. "Tonight, you'll see to it that I'm sated, won't you my love?"

He may have been speaking to Mireya, but he was watching Ryan.

"Yes, Roane. Whatever you want," she said.

He slid his hand under her shirt. Ryan didn't look up, but he froze. We all did. "You'll willingly do whatever I want, that's what I get for letting the cook live."

"For as long as you let him live."

"You do know how to please me, don't you?"

Mireya nodded.

Devlin massaged her breast. "Perhaps we should tie him up and let him watch."

"That's it!" Ryan dropped the spoon. By the time I'd stood, he'd already rounded the island. I blocked his path.

"Let me by!"

"No."

"Get the fuck out of my way!"

"No!"

I saw it coming and made no move to defend myself. The poor bastard needed to hit someone. The right cross landed square on my left cheek directly below my eye. No doubt I was going to have a shiner.

"Feel better?" I shouted.

Ryan shook out his hand. "I wanted to hit him!"

"Trust me, you don't. It's done. Let it go."

He couldn't. He tried to get past me again. If he made it, the shit was going to hit the fan. Devlin might have spared him in the end. But he'd have to teach Ryan a lesson and that lesson was going to leave him down for the count. I needed him at the top of his game. He'd made me a promise and I intended to see he kept it. One quick jab to the stomach, then an uppercut to the chin and Ryan was on the floor, gasping for breath.

The chair I'd been sitting in had gotten turned over in the scuffle. I picked it up and once again took my seat. "Allison, set the table for dinner. Ryan, when you've finished wheezing, you can start to serve."

"Asshole." He muttered it under his breath as he climbed to his feet.

"Sticks and stones," I replied. Allison had yet to move. She was studying me carefully, every eye movement, every breath, every twitch of every muscle. It would all mean something to her. I prayed to God she was paying attention and drawing the right conclusions.

"What are you waiting for?" I asked her.

She slowly pushed the chair back and rose from the table.

I waited until she'd rounded the island. "Hey, while you're up, fetch me a beer. Roane, would you like a beer?"

"I'd love a beer," he said, releasing Mireya and giving her a swat on the ass. "Go help Ryan with the salad."

Allison brought us two cold brews. I twisted the cap off mine and took a long pull.

"Your wolf is young, but strong. I sense potential in you," Devlin said.

Talking about me was the last thing I wanted to do. I'd hoped to use the time before dinner to somehow draw him out, to learn something useful, something I could later turn against him. The good ol' boys I was used to drinking beers with would have been content to let me steer the conversion to any number of subjects after a few minutes of talk about fucking, football or fishing. Apparently delusional heart-eating serial killers liked to be in charge.

I swallowed, then started to play along. "What kind of potential?"

Allison was setting the table. She placed a dinner plate and cutlery in front of me, then lingered long enough to hear Devlin's answer.

"The kind no one in this room could ever possibly understand…except for me."

"Don't listen to him, Jake. He—"

The rest of what Ryan was going to say to me was cut off.

"You promised!" shouted Mireya.

It happened so fast I hadn't even seen Devlin stand up. Ryan stumbled backwards, bumping into the oven. The knife

Allison had just placed on the table was now sticking out of his left thigh.

"He'll live," he said. "But it's going to be one sorry existence if he keeps pissing me off. Next time, I take it out on you. Understand?"

Mireya nodded.

"I will not have my authority undermined," Devlin continued. He looked around the room assessing each of our reactions before approaching Ryan.

"There won't be a next time. You have my word." Ryan gritted his teeth, pulled the knife out of his leg, and tossed it into the sink. Blood bubbled up out of the wound.

Devlin knelt in front of him. In a flash he'd ripped open Ryan's jeans, exposing the gash. "You smell delicious," he murmured.

"Let me put some pressure on it," Mireya had a clean dishtowel in her hand.

Devlin swept her aside. "I'm beginning to understand what you saw in him, my love. There's a certain..." He stood and moved in closer. Ryan was trapped between him and the refrigerator. Devlin rubbed up against him.

The hair on the back of my neck stood up.

Ryan closed his eyes.

Mireya turned away.

"...irresistible sweetness," continued Devlin. He licked his lips and ground his pelvis into Ryan's.

I slid quietly from my chair.

Allison held out her hand, signaling me to hold my position.

Ryan's hands were fisted at his sides. Whatever was going to happen, he was determined to let it. There was no way he was going to bring Devlin's wrath down on the woman he loved.

"You know what the smell of your blood makes me want to do?" Devlin asked him.

"No," Ryan managed to croak out.

From the looks of things it was going to be either feeding or fucking. The water that had been running upstairs turned off. Wright was finished with his shower. I glanced at the kitchen clock. How long did it take a kid to get dressed? Probably less time than it would take to satisfy a twisted son-of-a-bitch like Devlin. My mind was racing. I had to think of something and I had to think of it fast.

"Can you heal him?" asked Allison.

"What?"

"You heard me."

He held Ryan in place with one hand, but he took a step back and as far as I was concerned, that was a step in the right direction.

Allison folded her arms and leaned across the countertop. "Have you ever tried it before? Immortals can sometimes do it, right? It's how they prevent their mates from bleeding out. There's something in their saliva."

"There's something in a wolf's saliva too," Mireya interjected.

"But it's not as powerful." Devlin eased his way down Ryan's body until he was crouched in front of him, his mouth level with the seeping cut.

"Go on," encouraged Allison. "Lick it. Let's see what happens."

Devlin's tongue darted out and lapped at the wound. Ryan stood stock-still.

"Mmm," Devlin gazed up at Mireya and smiled, blood staining his chin and teeth. "He's tasty. We could share him later. Would you like that?" Devlin's eyes had changed. His voice was gravelly. His wolf was looking out at us and its strength made me shudder.

"Miranda?" He reached down and adjusted himself. When she didn't answer, he tugged on her hand, pulling her down onto the floor beside him. "Miranda!"

"The bleeding. It's stopped," she said, her voice echoing the disbelief I felt. "You stopped the bleeding in just a few seconds."

He looked at Allison. Then he stood and wiped his chin with the back of his hand. "I wonder if I could feed from, then heal a human?"

Mireya reached for Devlin's hand. "Allison isn't food. She's my friend. She's you're friend."

"I have no friends."

"She's going to help spread the word, bear witness to your power. Allison has...influence."

Devlin's brow furrowed. He scented the air. "Something's burning."

"The bread!" gasped Ryan. Obviously he was feeling better.

Devlin reached out and cupped the side of Ryan's face in the palm of his hand. "You've merely wet my appetite," he crooned. "Let's get dinner on the table. What do you say, Jake? Hungry?"

I clapped my hands, then rubbed them together. "You bet! I'm starved." Somehow I managed to sound enthusiastic instead of dumbfounded. I'd naively thought I'd bond with Devlin over a beer. From the looks of things, I should have slept with his wife and let him lick me. Shit, I didn't understand this guy at all.

Chapter Nineteen

"I never did like him, you know," Devlin said, with a nod toward Allison's hand. He popped the last bit of a dinner roll into his mouth and leaned back in his chair.

"In my opinion, a man who goes behind his wife's back and cheats on her isn't much of a man," he continued. "I thought you deserved better. Now you have the chance to have what I have." He gave Mireya's hand a squeeze.

"What you have," Allison repeated.

"Someone who is deserving of you. Jake here will grow into his paws. At the moment it might seem his wolf is too much for him to bear, but in time, with the right guidance..."

I leaned forward, expectant. Allison thrummed her fingers on the table.

Devlin took a sip of his wine. "At any rate, things seem to be working out just as I envisioned. Here we are, Doctor."

"You expect me to believe you told me about Gavin so I'd leave him, to come here, to be here, now?"

"Yes." He nodded. "Why else?"

"Power. Control. Dominance," she replied. "You wanted me weakened, distracted."

Devlin sat up. "You think you understand me? You think you know how my mind works? You have no idea."

"Enlighten me."

"You couldn't begin to understand, to see as I see, to know what I know, to become what I've become. This is just the beginning."

I was holding my breath, watching Allison work. All throughout dinner she'd been drawing him out, peeling back the layers and one by one revealing them to me.

"The beginning of what?"

Devlin leaned back in his chair. "That's the million-dollar question, isn't it? The one you've been trying to figure out since the day we first met."

"What's the end game here, Roane?"

"If this is a game, it's one I was predestined to play."

"And deadly serious. There have been many sacrifices."

"There are going to be more. It's inevitable. I supposed some might even consider it unfortunate."

Allison pushed the food on her plate around some more. She'd hardly eaten. "Not you?"

"I told you before, I'm prepared to sacrifice a few for the salvation of many."

"Salvation."

"Yes."

"So, in the final tally, when the last die is cast, what will we be left with?"

"A new race," Devlin said. "The one that was meant to be."

Mireya had started to clear the table. She was reaching for his dinner plate when he stopped her.

"The one we'll give birth to," he finished, placing his hand ever so gently on top of Mireya's stomach. "Soon," he murmured. "Very soon."

"I've been thinking, Roane. We should go," Mireya said. She was looking across the table at Ryan when she said it, her eyes filled with unshed tears.

"Go?"

She turned her full attention back to him. "We should go now, before the other members of the pack come back, before they find you. There's no point to staying here. To risking—"

Roane released Mireya. "The others won't be coming back." He reached for the bottle of wine in front of him.

"What did you say?" Mireya asked.

A sickening feeling developed in the pit of my stomach.

Devlin poured himself another glass of merlot, then set the bottle down. "This pack is mine."

"Roane, what did you do?"

He shrugged. "I removed an obstacle, my love."

Mireya paled. For a moment I thought she was going to faint. "You killed Dakota and Samuel? They're...dead?"

"Very," he replied, before draining the last of the wine. "I'd love to go into detail, but I wouldn't want to ruin anyone's supper."

Ryan pushed back from the table and ran to the door. Mireya moved to follow, but Roane stopped her.

"Let him be," he said. The sound of Ryan's retching floated back into the kitchen. For the second time in his young life, Ryan had lost his family. My own stomach churned. Samuel and Dakota were gone. They weren't coming back. They wouldn't be adding to our numbers. They wouldn't be coming to the rescue.

Devlin chuckled. "They put up a fight, I'll have to give them that. The older one was surprisingly strong. His wolf sensed me coming. The younger one was strong, but not ruthless enough.

He hesitated. This one..." He nodded toward the door. "He's weak, nothing more than a plaything."

Allison placed her hand on my knee. "I'm sorry, Jake."

Her voice seemed far away, the sounds of Ryan's cries of grief further still.

"At least these two have potential," Devlin said. "They're young, malleable." He looked across the table at Wright.

The boy's eyes were wide with fear. He was shaking. Dakota had taken him in and given him a home. He'd been kinder and more loving to Wright than the boy's real father.

"You remind me of myself when I was your age," Devlin continued. "Oh, the stories I could tell you. The things I could show you. The power I could give to you. It's out there, you know." He leaned forward and whispered, "It's out there for the taking."

At least a dozen options ran through my head. I didn't have the background Allison did, but by now there was one thing I was certain of, if Devlin stayed in this house more would be killed. Mireya's instincts were right. We had to get him out and out fast.

"The PSF will be here in the morning," I said it casually, as if it were of little consequence. Then I added, "You don't have much time."

"How do you know?" he asked.

"They've been shielding your mate. That's why tracking her was such a problem. Something happened, a malfunction. The shields came down for a time. They were here, just last night. They fixed them. But you'd already found Dakota and Samuel by then and picked up her scent."

Roane played with his glass, turning the stem back and forth slowly between his thumb and index finger. "All I had to do was track them back."

"So you followed them, stalked them?"

"Until I was certain. I attacked as they neared their truck. Miranda's scent was all over it. It was fresh." He closed his eyes. "Sweet." You would have thought he was remembering his grandma's peach pie. He turned to me. "The address on the registration led me here. The PSF won't be back."

"The agent they sent to warn us was a mage. He said a relocation team would arrive in the morning. You need to make your move tonight. It's not safe for you here," I told him.

"Why tell me?"

This was going to be the tricky part. I was going to get one shot and I needed to play it exactly right. Devlin didn't just want immortality, he wanted to be a father. His maker, like mine, had taken his life away from him. This was his chance to get it back, not only for him, but for all of us. He wasn't talking about fathering a child, he wasn't talking about leading a pack. No. Devlin was talking about restoring our race to what he believed was our intended place. Alone in his delusion, there was something he wanted, needed desperately. A disciple. Someone to spread the gospel. I had to convince him that someone was me.

I stood and carried my plate to the sink. "Why? I've been asking myself that very question since the day I was turned. Why me? Why this pack?" I began to pace back and forth, wearing a path between Devlin and the front door. Agitated, I continued and the words spilled out. "Why is Byron Renfield so interested in having me sign up for his special training program?"

"Renfield wants you to join the Academy?"

I nodded. The last bit left me breathless. My mouth was dry, the palms of my hands clammy. I wiped them on the sides of my jeans. "I had a dream." I said it quietly, almost to myself.

"A dream?" Devlin rose up out of his chair and walked toward me.

I stood there, rooted to the spot, my back to the door. "Before you came here, you came to me in a dream. At the time I didn't understand. Maybe I wasn't ready to believe."

"And now you are," he said.

"I'm...not sure."

"You are," Devlin insisted as he approached, his gaze penetrating. He placed his hand over my chest. "Stop thinking with your head. Think with your heart."

My heart. The nightmare I'd had was still fresh, its violent imagery flashed before me. I was standing now in the very spot I'd been standing in then. This time, the real monster was before me. My heart was pounding, my pulse racing, it was all I could do to keep my breathing steady and not pull away.

Devlin tilted his head to the side. Was he listening to the rush of my blood, trying to gauge my sincerity, or the supposed whispers of the Morning Star? I wasn't sure. I waited patiently for him to continue.

"The heart wants what the heart wants," he murmured to no one and everyone.

I held my breath.

He looked me in the eye. "Tell me, what does your heart want?"

A chair scraped back. It had to have been Allison. I couldn't stop. I couldn't look at her. I was committed. I had to press forward.

"Something it can't have," I admitted. "Something I lost and can never recapture."

Devlin smiled. My answer seemed to please him. "Your humanity. I understand. I understand all too well."

"Jake." Allison's voice carried a hint of warning.

"He wants to be a real boy again, Doctor."

"That's impossible," Allison argued.

"Is it?" Devlin asked. "Are you sure?"

Allison stepped forward. "Don't listen to him."

"Perhaps we can help one another, Jake," Devlin suggested.

She grabbed hold of my arm. "There's no cure for lycanthropy."

"Immortality cures everything," Devlin countered. "I can give that to you."

"Jake, look at me," Allison snapped.

I didn't. I couldn't. I kept my eyes focused on Devlin, the man who would lead me, the man who was going to show me the way to salvation.

"He's tempting you with something he can't deliver." She was tugging on my arm now, trying her damnedest to draw my attention.

Devlin seemed almost amused. "Oh, I can deliver it. The question is will Jake be willing to pay the price?"

"Let's say he can. Let's say he can make you immortal, that's not the same as being human," Allison reasoned.

"No," I agreed, barely sparing her a glance. I let a few seconds pass, before adding, "It's better."

Mireya joined Allision, her alarm was growing. "Leave him alone, Roane. Let's go, now. Just the two of us," she offered. "It's what you want, right? Just you and me."

Ryan was at the door, trying to get back inside. It was now or never.

"I can get you Renfield," I blurted out.

I had Devlin's rapt attention. "Byron Renfield?"

"Yes. He gave me some time to consider his offer. There's a window of opportunity, but we'll have to move fast. I can get us in."

"How?"

"I've been to his house. I know the layout. I know his children, his wife. All I have to do is call and tell him I've reconsidered."

"Renfield," Devlin whispered, his tone reverent. "He has great power."

"I want something in return."

"I know what you want."

"Do we have an agreement?"

He turned to Mireya and grabbed hold of her. "Everything is falling into place," he hissed. "The time is now. We must go."

"Okay," she eagerly agreed.

Devlin pushed me aside and opened the door. Ryan stood on the threshold, his eyes red from tears. He wasn't of any consequence to Devlin now. Perhaps he never was.

"Can you hear it?" Devlin walked right past Ryan, listening intently to something only he could hear. The wind whipped through the trees, flakes of snow now mixed with rain poured down from the sky. Devlin seemed oblivious, singularly focused he stepped off the porch.

"Teach me to listen," I said, following closely.

Heedless of the cold, my new master fell to his knees. Arms outstretched, head thrown back, he looked up into the light of the full moon and opened up his mouth. A howl poured out into the night. It floated across the clearing and bounced back off the mountains beyond. Echoes carried the sound back to us, multiplying it ten-fold, surrounding us in a spine-chilling chorus.

During the hunt we howl to scare our prey, to flush them out. It was a signal, a warning and without thought I joined Devlin, answering his call. My wolf began to pace back and forth inside its cage. It wanted out. It wanted to be free, to run wild.

"Jake!" I was aware Allison was calling to me, reaching for me. She was crying, begging me to stop, to come back to her. I couldn't stop and didn't want to. I unlocked the door and let myself go, embracing the power within me. Arms open wide, I tilted my face up and for the first time, truly allowed myself to bask in the power. I soaked it up and rolled with it, letting it wash over me, relishing instead of resenting the way it made me feel.

The crescendo built, our bays mixing with those reflecting off the mountains until the cries filled my head and shut everything else out. I could become one with the night. I was the darkness. Nothing would be able to stop me. Nothing. Unless I stopped myself.

Allison slapped me across the face. It was a stinging blow, but the look of fear and panic in her face stung worse. For a moment I wished I could reassure her. I wished I could explain. I wished for a lot of things but did none of them. Instead I grabbed her by the shoulders and pushed her away toward Ryan. He caught her as she stumbled.

"Jake!" She cried out, struggling against him, kicking and screaming.

Ryan was strong, his resolve steadfast.

I reached for Mireya. "It's time to go."

"What are you doing? Have you lost your mind?" She pulled away. "Ryan, control him!"

Only it was too late for that. Ryan had his hands full and even if he didn't, I knew and he knew I was stronger, more powerful than he was. Ryan couldn't control me. I was pretty sure Mireya couldn't either, but she was going to try. I was counting on that fact and she didn't disappoint me.

She faced me head on, her expression grave, her own power growing until it coursed through her in an almost palpable way. I felt it in the air.

"Go back in the house," she demanded.

There was no way I was going to go back in the house, not until this was finished.

"No. I'm coming with you."

"Go back in the house!" This time she placed her palms against my chest and pushed me.

I stumbled back a few steps before regaining my footing. Then with a roar I returned the favor. I had no choice, I told myself as I ran at her, shoulder down. A part of me always knew it would come to this between us. Mireya was a survivor. She was a good Beta, a good guide, but she wasn't a leader. A leader sometimes had to be brutal, show no mercy, make tough choices. And then live with himself and the consequences.

I heard a rib crack as I connected with her. Not one of mine, one of hers. The force of the blow propelled Mireya into the air. She came down about fifteen feet away, landing flat on her back in the snow. She was momentarily stunned, the wind knocked out of her, but she was resilient. The girl was used to being knocked around. She bounced back quickly.

In one fluid motion she rolled onto her side and was up on all fours, a low growl emanating from her chest. Her beast was rising. She was calling its power. If she dared risk tapping into her mate's, I was finished. Before she was able to transform or climb to her feet I was on her.

We tumbled and rolled. We were covered in snow. Our clothes were soaked from the rain. She kneed me, just missing my groin. The hit was close enough it made me falter. I made the mistake of wavering. It was merely for an instant. That instant cost me.

Mireya sprang up, teeth bared, ready to fight. She'd been waiting for an opening, hoping to gain an advantage. She was one up, I had to knock her back down.

I ran at her again. Leaping into the air, I dove and missed.

She was ready for me. As I sailed past her she kicked out, grazing the side of my knee. I landed face down. The cold, wet snow filled my ears and nostrils.

"Stand down!" she growled.

I wiped the snow from my eyes. The forward momentum of the fall had carried me further still from the house and Mireya followed.

"No!"

She pounced on top of my back.

The wolf inside me raged, refusing to give in, give up. She'd dominated it before. It wasn't going to let that happen again. Somewhere within the dark recesses of my being, it reared back on its haunches, prepared to attack. It broke into a run, its gait swift and sure. I felt it coming closer, closer. My legs were scrambling, digging in the snow, searching for something. I needed leverage. Somehow, I managed to pull my knees up beneath me. The beast flung itself against its cage. I arched up, absorbing its power. With a roar, I threw Mireya off.

She landed, hard.

I gave her time to get back on her feet. The tides had turned. We were nearing the end. We were almost in position.

"I won't lose to you this time," I shouted out over the din of the storm before launching myself at her.

Mireya took off at a run, but she wasn't fast enough. This time we connected and both went down.

I tangled my fingers into her hair and pulled her to me. "Trust me," I managed to whisper into the shell of her ear before Devlin approached.

"Enough!" He pulled me off, tossing me aside like a rag doll before scooping Mireya up and depositing her on her feet.

"I don't want him—"

Devlin was furious. "He will come with us," he shouted. "He is the key that will open the final door."

"But—"

"End of discussion!"

A gunshot rang out. The bullet whizzed past us, missing its target, just like it was supposed to.

I looked back. Ryan stood on the porch, rifle against the support post. Allison and Wright were tucked safely behind him. His face was filled with determination. He wasn't going to let me down. He was prepared to do what needed to be done.

"Run for the woods!" I shouted. "Once we're under cover we can shift."

Devlin turned to Mireya. "Do as he says!"

Only it was clear he wasn't going to run. He was going to stand his ground.

Ryan stepped off the porch. He ejected the empty shell, pulled back the bolt, and chambered another round as he moved nearer, step by resolute step.

Mireya took off. Whether it was because she was listening to me or listening to Devlin, I didn't care. She was heading toward the woods, away from the danger zone, and that's what mattered.

Ryan's next shot was deliberately too high, or so I thought. Then he moved closer still and I realized it wasn't deliberate at all. His aim was imprecise, his grip unsteady. In order to compensate, he was trying to get closer to his target. Problem was, every step was bringing him closer to peril. Whether it was the anger, grief, or just plain not caring, he seemed to have forgotten that.

Another shot rang out. I sprang past Devlin, running the fastest sprint of my life straight for Ryan. My stride was long, my speed so swift I practically skimmed across the surface of the snow. Ryan barely had the time to chamber the next round before I reached him.

"No!" Allison screamed.

I was sailing through the air, my hand reaching out. The second it connected with the cold barrel of the gun Ryan let go. Momentum carried me past him. I led with the weapon. My body twisted. I landed firmly on my feet, my stance perfect. I had the rifle's butt jammed into my right shoulder, sight at the ready. The barrel of the gun was pointed directly at Ryan.

Applause rang out from behind me.

Clap. Clap. Clap.

"Nicely done!" called out Devlin appreciatively.

I glanced up. Mireya was at the edge of the woods. She paused and turned, a look of horror on her face. I barely had time to register it.

"No!" Her blood-curdling scream almost drowned out Devlin's ongoing cheers.

Clap. Clap. Clap.

"Now, finish it!" he ordered. I had no choice but to follow his command.

I swung the weapon around, left hand under the barrel, right hand on the trigger. I closed my eyes, inhaled, then opened them. After letting out a partial breath, I took a bead on the target. Then ever so slowly, I squeezed the trigger.

Did Devlin look surprised? I'll never know.

The recoil of the rifle was nothing compared to the force of the blast as the snowman exploded. Ryan and I were both thrown off our feet. My ears were ringing, my head spinning as a rush of slush rained down on me. As soon as my head started to clear I rolled onto my side, pushed myself up, and surveyed the damage.

"Jesus!" gasped Ryan.

I'd never seen anything like it. Devlin was nowhere. And everywhere. Bits and pieces scattered like a macabre Pollock painting across the white canvas of the snow.

There was a large, gaping hole where the ANFO had been. Beyond it I could see Mireya. She was in wolf form and racing across the clearing. Ryan was next to me. He'd managed to pull himself to a sitting position.

I stood and offered him my hand. He was still shaky, we both were, but with help he managed to climb to his feet.

"You all right?" I asked.

He immediately started to shed his clothes. "I think I dislocated my shoulder."

I helped him off with his shirt.

"Something must've hit you." He gestured toward my forehead. "You're bleeding."

Within a matter of seconds he'd shifted.

"Go to her," I told him. "I'll be there in a second."

"Jake!"

Allison practically flew off the porch. She was running toward us, Wright at her side. Then suddenly, she was in my arms.

"I thought I'd lost you." The words came out in a rush as I lifted her off the ground.

"I'm right here," I whispered, holding her close. "I'm okay. Everything's okay."

Her heart beat against mine, steady and sure. I lowered Allison to the ground and let her go.

"Is it?"

For a long moment I just stood there, knee deep in snow, looking up at the moon. Big white flakes were still falling from the sky, drifting down and dancing around us.

"Is it really okay?" she asked.

In a few hours the evidence of the horror would be hidden beneath a pristine blanket. But it would still be there. It would always be there, just as my beast would always be there, lurking below the surface.

I'd told Allison there would be no more lies between us. She'd said she didn't want me making promises that couldn't be kept. So where did that leave us? She was seeking reassurance. Although I wanted to give it, I didn't. The truth was I had no idea what the future would bring, what my place in the world was going to be.

"Maybe not your run-of-the-mill happily-ever-after okay. But I'm here. You're here. The bad guy's gone. That's good enough for me. Good enough for now," I said.

Mireya and Ryan were at the edge of the clearing. Their howls drifted back on the wind, beckoning to me. They were telling me there were loose ends to tie up and a ritual to attend to. Samuel and Dakota were still out there, somewhere. They needed to be laid to rest.

"They want to search for Samuel and Dakota," I explained.

Wright had already stripped and was on his way to join them.

"The danger's gone. The storm is breaking. Go." Allison reached up and began to unbutton my shirt.

"What about you?" I asked her, stepping out of my jeans. "I don't want to leave you, not now." Hell, not ever.

"I'll be waiting for you inside, where it's warm."

Of course, she was freezing.

"I thought the hero was supposed to ride off into the sunset *with* the heroine?"

"Not tonight," she whispered, reaching up and brushing my hair back, out of my eyes. "Not in this world."

"No?" I asked, wrapping my arms around her and for a moment sharing my warmth. I leaned in to kiss her.

"No." Her lips were just a hairsbreadth from mine. "In this world, the heroes run naked through the woods and howl at the moon."

Epilogue

Six months later

Allison was even more beautiful than I remembered. I sat in the back row of one of the large lecture halls of Draper Hall, anxiously tapping my pencil on the blank sheet of paper in front of me while I once again checked the clock. Time had never moved so slowly. She paced in front of the class as she lectured, her eyes occasionally searching out mine.

It had been six excruciatingly long months since I'd seen her. Six months since we had decided to do the sensible thing, to part ways, to get some distance. At least it seemed sensible at the time. We would meet back at the ranch next spring, a year from the date I'd rescued her. That was the plan we agreed to. If what we had was real, it would be there in a year, she'd said. I believed her. And I wanted it to be real enough that I went along with her request.

So, I returned to school. Threw myself into my studies. Found and joined a local pack, a much larger one, in the Waco area. And tried not to think of her, the way she felt, the way she smelled, the way her mouth tasted. I was miserable.

Summer came and I went back to intern for my uncle in Dallas. My spare time was spent searching for Allison. I just wanted to hear her voice, I told myself. I wouldn't push. I wouldn't beg.

I needn't have bothered. There wasn't an Allison Connelly to be found teaching anywhere in southern California. I was on the verge of asking a private investigator my uncle used from time to time to hunt her down when Ryan talked me out of it.

"Give her the time she asked for. Take the time you need."

"That's easy for you to say. You have Mireya. The two of you are deliriously happy."

"All I'm saying is there's no need to rush things. You and I are both young."

I knew Ryan well enough to know there was something he wanted to say, something he wanted to talk about, but he was skirting the issue.

"You think the age difference between Allison and I—"

"Nah." He dismissed that concern with a wave of his hand. "It's... Mireya wants us to have a baby."

"Yeah?" I couldn't help but smile. "You'll make a terrific father."

"I don't know, Jake."

"You're doing all right by me. You know, I've always been the little brother. It'd be fun to be the big brother."

"There's a lot to consider. It's complicated."

"Actually, not so much. Winter's coming, the little guys will be swimming with purpose. From what I understand, they do all the heavy lifting. You just do what you normally do. I can sketch you some diagrams if you'd like."

"Between the two of us, I'm the one getting laid on a regular basis."

I sighed. "Yeah. How sad is that?"

"Maybe you should consider seeing someone."

"It's not like I'm suicidal. It's..."

"What?"

"I miss her."

"I know you do, buddy. I know."

The bell rang. I snatched up the pad of paper and pencil in one hand, my backpack with the other and took off down the stairs. I weaved my way through the throng of students. By the time I made it to the front of the lecture hall she was gone.

I pushed through the door. The area was filling up quickly. Young men and women were pouring out into the hallway, some lingering to chat, others scurrying off to catch their next class. I didn't care about them. All I cared about was catching up to her. I looked left first, then right.

"Allison!" I shouted. Several of my fellow students turned around. Allison didn't.

She was at the end of the hall, close to the stairs. There was no way she could outrun me, no way she could elude me. I'd been breathing her in for the last ninety minutes. I knew the scent of her soap. I knew the scent of her perfume. But most importantly, I knew the scent of her arousal and just how deeply I stirred the desire in her still.

I followed her down the stairs and around the corner. When I caught up with her she was standing at a door, keys in hand. Only her hand was shaking and she fumbled at the lock. I walked up behind her. The placard next to the door had her name on it.

"Allison?" I said it quietly. "Hand me the keys, I'll unlock the door. You're shaking."

She'd faced one of the most dangerous and demented of serial killers, but unexpectedly running into me had her in a tailspin.

"You said you were from Dallas," she whispered, not turning around. "You said you were a lawyer."

Was she afraid to face me? Had her feelings changed? Just as I was about to ask, the key slid into the lock. One turn and she opened the door and slipped inside.

"You lied to me." She sounded as if she were on the verge of tears. Before she had a chance to close the door in my face, my boot was there. The same boots I'd had on when I climbed down that ravine six months ago.

"I said I worked for a law firm in Dallas. It was true. Both last summer and the one before. I worked for my uncle in Dallas. I never said I was a lawyer, I'm sure of it. I'm going to be one, it's what I've always wanted to do, but I'm not one yet. Why would I lie about that?"

"I don't know." If I knew Allison, she was already replaying the conversations we'd had in her head.

"Let me in. People are going to wonder—"

That did it. She stepped back and I slid inside, closing the door behind me. The office was small, just big enough for a couple bookshelves, a desk, and two chairs. There were no windows and only the one door. Allison backed up slowly. I matched her step for step until she was pressed flat against the wall.

"I can't believe this is happening," she whispered, closing her eyes.

"Believe it," I said, taking another step toward her.

"You can't be a college student."

I smiled and wagged my finger at her. "You said you taught at a college in southern California. That wasn't exactly the truth, was it? I called every one. None of them had a professor Connelly."

"Connelly is my maiden name, Jake. Gavin's last name was Robinson. When I applied for the job at State, mine was as well. I hadn't changed it back yet."

That made sense. I cursed myself for not considering she might have continued to use her ex-husbands last name professionally for a while.

"A friend mentioned over lunch his next class was with a new professor, Allison Connelly. I was afraid to believe it was you. I didn't dare hope—"

"I was offered this job at the last minute," she explained, "when Deborah Marshall decided not to come back from maternity leave."

She paused to lick her lips. She glanced over my shoulder at the door. The hallway was still bustling, the chorus of voices blending together until they were indistinguishable from one another.

"How old are you, Jake?" she asked.

The question caught me off guard. I didn't want the age difference to matter. Suddenly it seemed like a very real possibility that it might. "I'm twenty-one. I'll be twenty-two in a few weeks."

"Twenty-one," she repeated.

"Yes, ma'am," I said, placing my hands on the wall on either side of her. I wasn't going to walk away, not now, and not without a fight. "Now, shut up and kiss me."

She reached out and placed her hand on my chest. For a second I thought she was going to push me away, but she didn't. I stood there stock still, holding my breath. Her hand trailed down over my stomach.

"I never should have let you in this door," she said, her voice breathless.

Had she been yearning for me, craving me, as much as I had her?

"You shouldn't have let me in the door? I never should have let you go. You weren't gone five minutes before I regretted it. It was the stupidest thing I've ever done."

"Jake—"

"I'm serious. You have no idea how much I've missed you. I've longed to hear your voice, feel your touch, breathe in your scent until I ached inside."

"I want you—"

"You want me, I'll give you that..." I murmured, my mouth hovering right above hers. I took her hand in mine and slid it down over the bulge in my jeans. I wanted her to know, to feel the effect of the power she held over me.

A sigh of longing escaped her lips.

"Kiss me," I demanded. Deftly I moved one of her hands around to the back of my neck and the other around my waist.

"You're a student. I can't."

"Sure you can."

"It's wrong," she protested weakly.

I stepped closer still, needing desperately to convince her of the opposite. That in fact, nothing had ever quite been so right. If the separation had taught me one thing, it was that I didn't want a life apart from hers. I didn't care if it was going to be messy, I didn't care if it was going to be complicated.

"So quit."

"Quit?"

"Or I'll quit."

"You can't quit school."

"Technically, I'm not your student. I'm not signed up for the class. Our relationship pre-dates you coming here. No one can accuse you of anything," I reasoned.

"You're being naïve. A few days of good sex—"

"Now, hold on a minute. I seem to remember it being great, mind-blowing sex," I corrected.

She smiled. "Okay, great, mind-blowing sex. That's...not a relationship."

"Right. I remember that argument. That's the one you used to get me to agree to the cooling-off period. It's been six months." I let my hand glide down over her hip, past her thigh. "If I have to go another six months, I'm going to self-combust. I swear."

She grabbed my wrist, stalling my progression. "Are you telling me you haven't been with anyone else?"

"Have you been listening to me? I don't want anybody else. I want you. Six more months, hell six more years of celibacy won't change that."

"I never asked you to be celibate. I didn't expect... What are you doing?"

I'd gathered up a handful of her hair and breathed it in, letting my lungs fill with the aroma before moving in to nuzzle the space just behind her ear that I so loved to kiss. Her skin was soft and smooth, even smoother than I remembered. The scratch of my emerging beard scraped across her jaw line slightly as I pulled back, to make my descent. I moved down the length of her neck, the hollow of her throat, over the exposed portion of collarbone.

"What—"

"Shh." I held her hips in place, my hand on them as I passed over her full, ripe breasts. "I'm concentrating."

I fell to my knees in front of her. Like most women, she was covered with lotions and potions. There was shampoo, soap, hand lotion, traces of face powder, even laundry detergent to contend with, but underneath it all, she still smelled like home, she still smelled like me. The time, the distance, nothing had erased, nothing could disguise the fact that she still belonged to me.

I let my hands glide over the contours of her body, my fingertips just grazing her ass, the backs of her thighs. Her neck and chest were flush with arousal. Her breath hitched. Her head leaned back. She stared up at the ceiling and licked her lips.

My detailed exploration of her was almost sinfully self-indulgent. But I'd done it unabashedly, like a dog marking his territory. This was territory I knew well and I considered it mine. "Have you cooled off, Allison?"

"No."

"No?" I gingerly gathered up the edge of her skirt. She was wearing stockings. That was new. I traced the tops of them, teasing.

"No." Her heart was pounding, pumping blood into all the right places. Mine was too. I was rock hard and in serious need of release. "But—"

I climbed to my feet and placed a finger over her mouth, silencing her.

"I listened to you back then. It's your turn to listen to me now. You hear me?"

She nodded and I removed my hand.

"I hear you," she murmured. Her mouth now tantalizingly close to mine.

"Maybe what we had last spring wasn't a relationship," I agreed, brushing my lips across hers, my tongue darting out to tease her bottom lip. "But it was something and it could be more. I want it to be more."

"More?"

"Much, much more. Maybe even a great beginning."

"Beginning of what?"

"Something serious. Something lasting. Something permanent."

"Jake—"

"Come on, Allison. Don't push me away. You winding up here at Baylor? It's more than coincidence. I love you."

"I love you, too," she whispered without a moment's hesitation.

"Then don't let this chance pass us by. People wait their entire lives for the right person to come along. What if you're it? What if I'm it? I know you're afraid of getting hurt again. I know I'm asking you to take a big risk here but I'm not Gavin and—"

"Jake?"

"Yes?"

"Shut up and kiss me."

"Oh, darlin', I'm going to do more than that and you know it," I promised as I lifted her up and laid her across the polished mahogany desk. "I'm going to do much, much more than that."

About the Author

Samantha Sommersby lives in San Diego with her husband and teenaged son. She is the author of multiple novels and novellas including the critically acclaimed *Forbidden* series. In 2007 Samantha left what she used to call her "real life" day job as a psychotherapist to pursue writing full-time. She now happily spends her days immersed in the world of the *Forbidden*, a world where vampires, werewolves and demons are real, where magic is possible, and where love still conquers all.

To learn more about Samantha Sommersby, to follow her on Myspace, Facebook, Twitter, or Yahoo, or to sign up for her monthly newsletter, visit www.samanthasommersby.com. You may contact the author through her website or by sending an email to samantha@samanthasommersby.com.

LaVergne, TN USA
22 December 2010
209796LV00010B/1/P